As soon as Matt had left for work Rachel got dressed and drove into town to buy a pregnancy testing kit.

She took it back to her own home and did the test there. Waiting for the results was agonising, but finally she had confirmation that her suspicions were correct. She was pregnant, and now she needed to decide what she was going to do.

How she was going to tell Matt was also something she still hadn't worked out. It would have been different if they had made a real commitment to each other, but their relationship was founded on the here and now, and she certainly wouldn't *blackmail* him into staying with her because of their child.

Matt had a highly developed sense of duty, and she knew that he would feel he had to support her if they were still together when she broke the news to him. She couldn't bear to think that he could end up resenting her one day. Tears stung her eyes but she really didn't have a choice.

It would be better to end things now than to run the risk of that happening.

Dear Reader

This is the fourth and final story in my *Dalverston Weddings* series, and I have to admit to feeling a little sad now that I have reached the end. However, helping my hero and heroine discover how much they love one another was a real joy for me—even though it did come as a shock to them!

Rachel Mackenzie and Matthew Thompson have worked together for a number of years, and they have an excellent working relationship based on mutual respect and liking. However, when the wedding of their respective offspring is suddenly cancelled, they find themselves taking a long, hard look at their own feelings and are stunned when they realise that they are attracted to one another. Both are wary of rushing headlong into a situation they might come to regret, and agree that an affair seems like the ideal solution—but will it be enough for either of them?

I hope you enjoy reading this book as much as I enjoyed writing it. I particularly loved planning the last scene, as it reminded me of my daughter's wedding day. I spent many happy hours looking through all the photographs in the name of research!

Best wishes to you all

Jennifer

THEIR
BABY SURPRISE

BY
JENNIFER TAYLOR

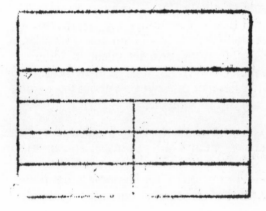

⦿™ MILLS & BOON®

First published in Great Britain 2009
Large Print edition 2010
Harlequin Mills & Boon Limited,
Eton House, 18-24 Paradise Road,
Richmond, Surrey TW9 1SR

© Jennifer Taylor 2009

ISBN: 978 0 263 21098 9

Harlequin Mills & Boon policy is to use papers that are
natural, renewable and recyclable products and made
from wood grown in sustainable forests. The logging and
manufacturing process conform to the legal environmental
regulations of the country of origin.

Printed and bound in Great Britain
by CPI Antony Rowe, Chippenham, Wiltshire

Jennifer Taylor lives in the north-west of England, in a small village surrounded by some really beautiful countryside. She has written for several different Mills & Boon® series in the past, but it wasn't until she read her first Medical™ Romance that she truly found her niche. She was so captivated by these heart-warming stories that she set out to write them herself!

When she's not writing, or doing research for her latest book, Jennifer's hobbies include reading, gardening, travel, and chatting to friends both on and off-line. She is always delighted to hear from readers, so do visit her website at www.jennifer-taylor.com

Recent titles by the same author:

THE DOCTOR'S BABY BOMBSHELL*
THE GP'S MEANT-TO-BE BRIDE*
MARRYING THE RUNAWAY BRIDE*
THE SURGEON'S FATHERHOOD
  SURPRISE**

*Dalverston Weddings
**Brides of Penhally Bay

For the Wedding Party: Vicky and Jamie, Kathy, Carl, Pauline, John, Nigel, Neil, Mark, Mel. And, last but never least, Bill. Thank you all for an unforgettable day

CHAPTER ONE

HE MAY have been putting on a brave face all day but Rachel Mackenzie wasn't deceived. It was no secret to those who knew him that Matthew Thompson adored his only daughter, Heather, so the fact that Heather had decided to cancel her own wedding and leave Dalverston was bound to have caused him a great deal of pain.

Rachel sighed as she followed Matt into his house because it was painful for her too. It had been her son, Ross, who had been due to marry Matt's daughter that day and she couldn't begin to imagine how devastated Ross must be feeling.

'I don't know about you but I could do with a drink.' Matt led the way into the sitting room and went straight to the table under the window that held an array of bottles. Picking up a bottle of whisky, he glanced at her. 'Will you join me, Rachel?'

'All right, but just a small one.' Rachel grimaced as she sank down onto the sofa. 'I'm so exhausted that even a sip of alcohol will probably send me off to sleep.'

'It's been one heck of a day,' Matt concurred, pouring two small measures of whisky into a pair of cut-glass tumblers. He handed one of the glasses to her then sat down with a sigh that spoke volumes about how he was feeling. Rachel studied him while she sipped her drink.

Normally, Matt was so full of energy that he appeared far younger than his actual age. He ran the busy general practice that served the people of Dalverston with a verve that few could emulate. However, today every one of his forty-eight years showed in the deep lines that were etched onto his handsome face.

At a little under six feet tall, with a powerful physique and thick black hair that was only just starting to turn silver at the temples, Matthew Thompson was a very attractive man. Rachel knew she wasn't alone in thinking that either. Several of her friends, the married ones as well as the single, had remarked on it. In fact, she'd had a job to convince them that she wasn't interested in Matt *that* way and saw him simply as a colleague and a friend.

It was a good job, too, she thought suddenly. Quite apart from the fact that she wasn't interested in having a relationship with anyone at the moment, there was definitely no chance of it happening with Matt. The thought touched a nerve oddly enough and she cleared her throat, unsure why it should trouble her in any way.

'I couldn't believe it when you phoned and told me we had a major incident on our hands. I mean for it to happen today of all days…' She tailed off, not needing to explain why today had been the worst day possible. Instead of celebrating their children's marriage, they had spent a large part of the day dealing with the aftermath of a serious accident on the banks of the canal. Talk about bad timing wasn't in it.

'At least it provided a distraction.' Matt grimaced when he realised how uncaring that must have sounded. 'Sorry. I didn't mean that the way it came out. A number of people were badly injured when that crane collapsed and I certainly wouldn't have wished that on them.'

'I know you wouldn't, but you're right, Matt. At least while we were treating them, it took our minds off this other problem,' Rachel said quickly, not wanting him to feel bad about what he had said.

'Exactly.'

He gave her a tight smile as he raised the glass to his lips. Rachel knew that he rarely drank alcohol, and never during the day, and it just seemed to prove how low he must be feeling. The thought caused her such intense pain that it surprised her. It was only natural that she should feel upset for Ross, but that didn't explain why it was so painful to see the way Matt was suffering, did it?

Rachel wasn't sure what to make of it all. In the end, she decided not to worry about it. Ross had attended the incident along with the rest of the staff from the surgery and she wanted to make sure that he had got home safely. She hunted her mobile phone out of her pocket and stood up. Matt looked up and she felt an odd little frisson run through her when their eyes met.

'I just want to phone Ross and check he's all right,' she explained, trying to stem the shiver that was trickling so disturbingly down her spine. What bothered her most was that she couldn't remember the last time something like this had happened. She kept too tight a rein on her emotions to let them misbehave this way, but obviously recent events had taken their toll.

She had been looking forward to this wedding so much, looking forward to the fact that from here on her son would have the woman he loved by his side to support him. Although she had never met anyone she had wanted to spend the rest of her life with, she believed in marriage, firmly believed that a happy marriage was a wonderful thing.

Was it disappointment that all her hopes for her son's future had amounted to nothing that was making her feel so mixed up? she wondered suddenly. She certainly couldn't remember feeling so emotionally raw before and that could explain the odd way she seemed to be behaving that day.

'You do that while I make us some coffee.' Matt put his glass on the table and stood up. He shrugged as he took Rachel's glass from her and placed it next to his. 'I don't think alcohol is the answer somehow, do you?'

'Probably not.' Rachel summoned a smile as he passed her on his way to the kitchen, but she was aware that it was an effort to behave naturally. Knowing that she wasn't in control of herself as she usually was worried her, too. She certainly didn't want to make a fool of herself in front of Matt.

She sighed softly as she dialled Ross's number. She and Matt had a very good relationship, she'd always thought. They trusted each other in work and enjoyed an easy camaraderie outside the surgery. Recently they had been spending a lot more time together as they had helped their respective offspring finalise the plans for their wedding and she had found herself enjoying his company too. Was that when she had become more aware of Matt as a man and not solely as a colleague? Had those hours they had spent together altered her perception of him?

The thought troubled her. She wasn't sure if she wanted to make any adjustments to how she saw Matt. It seemed rather danger- ous to alter the status quo, unpredictable, and if there was one thing Rachel didn't handle well it was the unpredictable. She liked her life to have structure, lots of nice tidy com- partments to file away both people and events so she knew how to deal with them.

She frowned. It didn't sound a very appeal- ing way of living, did it? Nevertheless, it had worked all these years for her and worked well too. Maybe this wedding had thrown her off course but she mustn't allow it to affect her too much. Once she got over the shock of it being cancelled, hopefully her life would return to normal.

Matt plugged in the kettle then took a tin of ground coffee out of the freezer. He spooned some into the cafetière then stood staring into space while he waited for the water to heat. It was almost four in the afternoon and if the day had gone as planned, he should have been enjoying the reception now. He would have been gearing himself up for his speech, not that it would have been difficult as wishing Heather and Ross every happiness for their future together was something he had been looking forward to doing. He had been so sure that Heather had found her ideal partner but had it been wishful thinking on his part? Although Heather hadn't said so, was he guilty of pushing her and Ross into this marriage?

Matt had a horrible feeling it might be true.

He had been so pleased that Heather had found someone as reliable as Ross that he had overlooked the signs that the relationship maybe wasn't what it should have been. He had put his desire for Heather to have security above everything else and he regretted it now. Deeply.

Maybe he had sworn that he would make sure their daughter was safe after Claire, his wife, had died, but Heather needed more than security. She needed love, laughter, *fun*, and he wasn't sure if Ross could have provided her with all of those things.

The truth was there had always been that vital spark missing, now that he thought about it. That extra dimension needed to take a relationship up a level. He and Claire had had it and it was one of the reasons why he had never been able to imagine falling in love with anyone else. He didn't think any other woman could light that spark inside him again.

'Ross is back at home. He says he's fine, but I'm sure he's only saying that to stop me worrying.'

Rachel came into the kitchen. She gave a gusty sigh as she stared at her phone as though it should be able to tell her if her son was telling the truth, and Matt felt himself grow tense. He couldn't see her face clearly with her head lowered like that so maybe that was why she appeared different all of a sudden, almost like a stranger.

She looked up and his heart gave the oddest little jolt as he found himself taking stock of the familiar yet strangely unfamiliar features—the elegant little nose, the softly rounded cheeks, the lusciously full lips now gnawed clean of any trace of lipstick. She'd had her hair done for the wedding and the soft chestnut curls looked so invitingly silky as they tumbled around her face that he longed to touch them, feel their softness against the palms of his hands, the tips of his fingers, so tempting and alluring…

He took a deep breath and stamped down hard on that thought. There would be no stroking of hair going on here!

'Did Ross say if he'd heard from Heather?' he asked instead, picking up the kettle. He poured the hot water into the pot and pressed down the plunger, quite forgetting to let the coffee brew first.

'No. I didn't ask him, to be honest. Sorry.'

Rachel's pretty face filled with remorse and that odd feeling he'd had about her being a stranger immediately receded. Once again she was Rachel Mackenzie, a woman he liked and respected, and he breathed a little easier at finding himself back on familiar territory. It had been just a blip, he told himself as he took a couple of mugs out of the cupboard, a tiny aberration caused by the stresses of the day and definitely nothing to worry about.

'It doesn't matter. I'm sure Ross would have said if Heather had phoned him,' he said soothingly, filling the mugs with coffee and frowning when he saw how insipid it looked. 'This doesn't look too good. I'll make another pot.'

'It's fine. Don't worry about it.'

Rachel picked up one of the mugs and carried it over to the table. Matt's heart ached when he saw how upset she looked as she sat down. What had happened today had had a big effect on Rachel too and for some reason the thought upset him even more. It wasn't fair that someone as kind and as gentle as Rachel was should have to suffer this way.

He went to join her, trying to find the right words that, hopefully, would make the situation easier for her. 'I know how hard this must be for Ross but he'll get through it, Rachel, you'll see.'

'Do you think so?' She looked up and he

could see tears brimming in her huge brown eyes. 'I feel so helpless, Matt. Oh, I know Ross is a grown man and more than capable of running his own life, but he's still my son and I love him dearly.' The tears spilled over and trickled down her cheeks. 'I just can't bear to think of him hurting this way.'

'I know. And I understand how you feel, really I do.'

Matt reached across the table and squeezed her hand. Her hand was so small that his seemed to engulf it and it surprised him how it made him feel—overwhelmed with tenderness and a need to protect her. He cleared his throat but he could hear the roughness in his voice even if Rachel couldn't.

'It's a difficult time for both Heather and Ross but I'm sure they will work things out in the end.'

He withdrew his hand, unsure what was happening and why he felt this way. This was

Rachel, he reminded himself, someone he had worked with for a number of years, a trusted colleague as well as a friend. However, the description no longer seemed to fit as accurately as it had done in the past; there seemed to be an extra dimension to Rachel he had never noticed before.

He frowned because that wasn't quite true. If he was honest, his view of her had been changing for a while now. They had spent a lot of time together in recent months planning for the wedding and he had found himself looking forward to it too. She wasn't just a colleague and a friend any longer. He was very much aware that she was a woman as well and a very attractive woman too.

The thought stunned him. For the first time since his wife had died Matt realised that he was aware of another woman's femininity and he couldn't believe that the feelings he had believed long dead were very much alive.

His whole body suffused with heat all of a sudden because he was powerless to stop what was happening. When he looked at Rachel, sitting here at his table, what he saw, first and foremost, was a woman he wanted to put his arms around. A woman he wanted to make love to.

CHAPTER TWO

'SORRY. I know this is just as difficult for you as it is for me, Matt.'

Rachel plucked a tissue out of her pocket and wiped her eyes. The last thing she wanted to do was to make the situation even more stressful for Matt.

'There's nothing to apologise for,' Matt said swiftly, and she looked at him in dismay when she realised how strange he sounded. It wasn't that he sounded angry or even upset, just...*odd*.

'Are you all right?' she asked anxiously, leaning forward so she could get a better look at his face. It was early December and the nights soon drew in at this time of the year.

They hadn't switched on any lights and Matt's face was in shadow, making it difficult for her to see his expression clearly.

'Yes. Just a bit shaken by what's happened, I suppose,' he replied, and she was relieved to hear him sounding more like he usually did this time.

'You and me both. I was stunned when Ross told me this morning the wedding had been called off.' She gave a little sigh. 'I still find it hard to understand why it's happened, if I'm honest. I always thought he and Heather were a perfect match, didn't you?'

'Ye-es.'

Rachel frowned when Matt seemed to hesitate. 'That sounded almost as though you had your doubts. Did you?'

'Not before this happened, no. However, now I'm not so sure.'

He stood up and switched on the light then sat down again. Rachel could see a glimmer of some emotion in his green eyes that she found it difficult to interpret.

'You don't think their marriage would have worked?' she said slowly, struggling to digest the idea.

'The honest answer is that I don't know any more. I thought they were ideally suited too, but I was thinking about it while I was making the coffee and I realised there was always something missing, that spark which makes a relationship truly special.'

'Do you really think so?' she said in surprise.

'Yes, I do. I only wish I'd realised it sooner. I wouldn't have pushed them into getting married then.'

'You didn't push them, Matt!' she exclaimed. 'It was their decision and it had nothing to do with you or anyone else for that matter.'

'I wish I could believe that but I have a horrible feeling that I'm more than partly responsible for this mess.'

'Rubbish!' She glared at him when he looked at her in surprise. 'I'm sorry but that's exactly what it is—complete and utter rubbish. They're both old enough to know their own minds. It wouldn't have mattered a jot what you thought.'

'Let's hope you're right.' He gave her a quick smile although Rachel could tell that he wasn't convinced. Matt obviously blamed himself for what had happened and that must make the situation even more difficult for him.

There was little she could say to persuade him otherwise, however, so she let the matter drop, talking about what had happened down by the canal instead. They had treated at least a dozen people who had been injured in the accident and it was always useful to compare notes after the event. It was only when Rachel heard the hall clock strike the hour that she realised it was time she left.

'I'd better be off,' she announced, standing up.

'I'll run you home,' Matt offered straight away, following her into the hall. He had collected her in his car along with the rest of the team from the surgery and ferried them to the site of the accident, which was why Rachel didn't have her own car with her. However, as she lived only a ten-minute walk away she immediately protested.

'There's no need, Matt. I can easily walk home from here. There's no point dragging you out of the house.'

'No, it's dark outside and I don't want you walking down that lane on your own.' He took his coat off the hallstand before she could protest any further and she gave in. There was no point making an issue out of it, was there?

It took them a bare five minutes to drive to her home. She had bought the cottage when she had moved to Dalverston and had spent a lot of time and effort restoring it over the last few years. She had always loved the cottage's quirkiness and its sense of history, not to mention its location, backing onto the river. However, she had to admit that the sight of the darkened windows made her heart sink a little as they drew up outside.

Normally it didn't bother her that she lived on her own. She'd had Ross while she was still in her teens, getting pregnant the first time she had slept with her boyfriend. Ross's father had been just a year older than her, far too young to want to accept responsibility for the child he had fathered.

With her parents' help, Rachel had brought Ross up, working hard to give them both a good life. Getting through medical school had taken a huge amount of determination with a young child to care for but she had succeeded and it had got easier as Ross had grown older. However, one thing she had never factored into her busy life was time for a proper relationship.

She'd had a couple of affairs over the years, and still dated occasionally, but that was all. Although the few men she had been involved with had appeared perfect on paper, she had never been tempted to commit to a long-term relationship with any of them. Quite frankly, she hadn't had any inclination to fall in love with all its attendant pitfalls, especially not after her first disastrous experience. She had been perfectly happy with her life the way it was...

Or so she had thought.

Rachel's breath caught as the doubts slid into her mind. She had everything she had ever dreamed of having, a job she loved, a son she adored, a comfortable home, so what on earth could be missing? Surely she didn't wish that she had someone to come home to, someone who would be waiting for her with a smile and a hug?

'Here we are, then. Want me to come in with you and check everything's all right?'

Matt's voice mingled with her thoughts and Rachel had the craziest urge to shout, Yes, please! Please come in with me. Please stay and talk to me, share this evening and maybe share other evenings with me too, but she managed to stop herself in time. If she took the first step down that route, who knew where she would end up? The thought scared her.

'No, it's fine,' she said, hoping he couldn't hear the panic in her voice.

'Sure?' He stared at the darkened windows and frowned. 'I don't like to think of you going into an empty house on your own.'

'I'll be fine,' Rachel said firmly, as much for her own benefit as his. She grasped the door-handle, ready to get out of the car, then stopped when he suddenly leant across the seat and kissed her gently on the cheek. His lips were cool from the night air and she shivered when she felt them brush her skin, hastily blanking out the thought of how good it would feel if he kissed her properly on the mouth.

'Take care, Rachel. It's been a tough day for all of us. If you need someone to talk to, you know where I am.'

'I…um…thank you.'

Rachel scrambled out of the car and almost ran up the path to the front door. Her hands were shaking so hard that it took her a moment to fit the key into the lock. Stepping into the tiny vestibule, she switched on the porch light then turned and waved. Matt gave a toot on his horn and drove away, his tail-lights rapidly disappearing into the darkness, but it was several minutes before she closed the door and went inside.

She stood there in the hall, deliberately drinking in the peace and quiet of her home in the hope that it would calm her, but for some reason the magic didn't work that night. Instead of peace all she felt was loneliness, instead of soothing quiet, emptiness, and she bit her lip. She had thought she was happy with her lot but all of a sudden she was aware of all that she lacked. She may have a fulfilling job, good friends, a son she adored, but she needed more.

She needed someone to love her and hold her in the night. Someone she could love and hold onto too, but was it too late for that? She was forty-six years old and it seemed crazy to be wishing for more than she had, more than might be good for her. Did she really want to risk falling in love at this point in her life, always supposing she met someone to fall in love with. Suitable men weren't exactly thick on the ground.

A picture of Matt suddenly appeared in her mind's eye and she frowned. If she did fall in love, it would have to be with someone like Matt, someone she trusted and respected, someone she found attractive too. But where could she hope to find anyone like Matt? He was a one-off. Special. There wasn't another man like Matt in the whole wide world.

A tiny sigh escaped her as she went into the sitting room and turned on the lamps, filling the house with light. There was no point even *thinking* about falling in love with Matt when there was little likelihood of him reciprocating her feelings. The only woman Matt had ever loved was his late wife and she certainly couldn't compete with her.

'I'm sorry, Matt, but I've had to add a couple of extra patients onto your list. Rachel asked me if I'd try to make some cuts to Ross's list and it was the only way I could fit everyone in.'

'That's fine, Carol, don't worry about it. We'll just have to pull together until everything settles down.'

Matt smiled at the practice manager, hoping he hadn't visibly reacted at the mention of

Rachel's name. It was Monday morning and he had just arrived at the surgery. He had planned on getting there early that day but as luck would have it, he'd had a phone call from the Ambulance Control centre as he'd been about to leave home. By the time he had dealt with that, the traffic had built up in the town centre and he'd had the devil of a job getting through it. Now he had barely five minutes to spare before his first appointment.

'Oh, good, there you are, Matt. What happened? Did you oversleep?'

Matt turned when he heard Rachel's voice, trying to quell the tremor that ran through him when he saw her standing behind him. She was wearing what she normally wore for work—a tailored suit with a white blouse and low-heeled shoes. Today her suit was cherry-red, a colour that shouldn't have worked with her glorious chestnut hair, yet it did. The richness of the hue highlighted her porcelain-fine complexion and made her large brown eyes look darker than ever. She had chosen a slightly deeper shade of lipstick to complement it and the colour emphasised the fullness of her mouth.

Matt felt his stomach lurch as his gaze lingered on her luscious lips. He still didn't understand what was going on. For almost six years, six extremely *comfortable* years too, he had viewed Rachel as a colleague and a friend, but he could no longer think of her solely that way. Far too many times over the weekend he had found his thoughts returning to her and they had been thoughts he had never entertained before. The memory of them made him inwardly squirm and he hurried to reply. Rachel would run a mile if she discovered that he had been fantasising about her sharing his bed!

'Sorry I'm so late. Someone from Ambulance Control phoned as I was about to leave home.' He picked up the bundle of notes Carol had prepared for him and headed to his consulting room, talking to Rachel over his shoulder because it seemed wiser than doing so face to face. At least this way he wouldn't start fantasising about her gorgeous mouth again. 'That's what delayed me.'

'Did they want to know about what happened on Saturday?'

Rachel followed him along the corridor, quickening her pace to keep up with him. At a smidgen over five feet three, she was a lot shorter than he was even in heels. Matt's first instinct was to slow down but the need to curtail all this craziness was just too strong. He had to stop thinking of Rachel as a woman and remember that she was a colleague.

'Uh-huh. That's right.' He stopped when he reached his room, inwardly groaning when he realised that he couldn't keep avoiding looking at her. Rachel would think it very strange if she had to carry on talking to the back of his head.

He forced himself to smile as he turned to face her. This close he could smell her perfume and his nostrils twitched appreciatively as he inhaled the scent of jasmine mingled with something even more exotic, a fragrance that stirred his blood in a way it hadn't been stirred for years. As the father of a grown-up daughter, Matt was accustomed to the smells of the lotions and potions that women applied to themselves; however, he had to admit that he hadn't smelled anything as delicious as the perfume Rachel was wearing that morning. It was an effort to concentrate when his mind was intent on racing off down a completely different path.

'Ambulance Control want us to send them a detailed report of what we did once we arrived on scene,' he explained, taking a step back in the hope it would make life easier. It did, a bit, but he could still smell jasmine as well as that other fragrance, something exotic and spicy and wickedly sexy…

'It will need to be a joint effort, then, won't it?' Rachel stated, and Matt dragged his wayward thoughts back into line again. At least one of them was functioning with a clear head and he should be grateful for that.

'It will. Everyone did something different, plus we arrived separately too. Ross and Gemma were first on scene and they had already prioritised the casualties by the time we turned up.'

'How long was it before the rapid response unit got there—do you remember?'

Rachel frowned as she tried to recall the exact order of events and Matt sucked in his breath as he watched her brow pucker. When had a frown become so beguiling? he wondered in astonishment, then hastily blanked out the thought because he really and truly didn't want to know the answer.

'About fifteen minutes after us, although I think there was a paramedic car there before then. I'll have to check with Ross about that. He'll have a better idea than me.'

'I hope this isn't going to turn into a major investigation,' Rachel said anxiously. 'There's bound to be a bit of a hullabaloo because most of the rapid-response vehicles were off the road thanks to that problem they had with their fuel supply. That's probably why Ambulance Control want us to write a report. They will need to have a full picture of what went on. I don't want Ross dragged in if there's an inquiry, though. He's got quite enough on his plate at the present time.'

'I can't see why any of us should be involved to that extent,' Matt assured her, hating to hear her sounding so worried. He patted her arm then wished he hadn't done so when he felt his blood pressure soar. 'We'll keep our report as general as possible. There's no reason why individual members of our staff should have to account for their actions at this stage.'

'Good. I don't want to add to the pressure Ross is under at the moment. To be honest, I don't think he should be at work today. It's madness to try and carry on as though nothing has happened.'

'We'll do our best to lighten his load as much as we can,' Matt said soothingly. 'Carol said that you'd asked her to re-jig his lists so that should help. And if it gets too much for him then he must go home.'

'You wouldn't mind?' Rachel smiled in relief when he shook his head. 'Thanks, Matt. I know Ross thinks I'm fussing but I can't help worrying about him.'

'Of course you can't,' Matt replied, his innards doing cartwheels as he basked in the glow of her smile. He cleared his throat and forced himself to focus. 'Right, I'd better get ready before my first patient arrives and catches me on the hop.'

'Me too. There's nothing more offputting for a patient than watching their doctor scrabbling about, trying to find the right case notes. It doesn't exactly inspire confidence, does it?'

Rachel laughed as she hurried away, causing his insides to perform yet another tricky manoeuvre. Matt thankfully went into his room and closed the door, hoping it would provide some protection from what ailed him.

He sighed as he sat down behind his desk. What did ail him, though? Was it the shock of Heather cancelling her wedding and leaving Dalverston that was making him feel as though he was on some sort of emotional roller-coaster ride?

For eight long years, ever since Claire had died so tragically of a stroke, he had felt very little. Every thought, every fibre of his being, had been poured into looking after Heather. Caring for Heather had filled the void left by his wife's death, but now that Heather no longer needed him he had nothing to fill it with. Did that explain why he was suddenly experiencing all these desires and urges he had believed long dead?

Matt tried to tell himself it was that simple but in his heart he knew it wasn't true. He was merely papering over the cracks because he was afraid of what he would find if he delved too deeply. He had loved once and it had been the most wonderful experience of his life. He was too scared to try and repeat it, terrified that it could only end in disappointment. How could he ever hope to find another woman to replace Claire?

He couldn't because Claire had been unique, special. However, it didn't mean that there wasn't someone else equally special in her own unique way. Once again his thoughts returned to Rachel and a little tingle ran through him, like a frisson of static electricity passing over his skin. He could deny it till the moon turned blue but the truth was that Rachel definitely had an effect on him.

CHAPTER THREE

RACHEL heaved a sigh of relief as she sat down at her desk and switched on the computer. She had been dreading seeing Matt after what had happened over the weekend. Time and again she had found herself returning to the thought that he would never love anyone the way he had loved his late wife and it was so stupid to have let the idea upset her. She really couldn't understand why it had become such a big deal when she had always known how he felt.

In the whole time she had worked at Dalverston Surgery, Matt had never shown any interest in another woman. He never dated, never flirted, never even hinted that he was interested in the opposite sex. He had poured all his energy into his job and caring for Heather, and she had admired him for it too, so why had that admiration suddenly changed to concern? Was she reflecting her own emotional turmoil onto him?

Rachel wasn't sure if that was the real answer and it was unsettling to find herself dealing with uncertainties when she preferred absolutes. It was a relief when her first patient arrived and she could concentrate on her instead. Miss Bessie Parish was eighty years old, a spinster who had lived in Dalverston all her life. She was one of Ross's patients normally but she had agreed to see Rachel instead that day. Rachel invited her to sit down and asked her what she could do for her.

'I've not felt at all well lately, Dr Mackenzie,' Miss Parish replied in her forthright way. 'I had a nasty cold a couple of weeks ago and it's left me feeling very wheezy and breathless.'

'I see. Have you had a cough as well?' Rachel asked, picking up her stethoscope.

'Yes, and I've been bringing up phlegm too.'

Miss Parish's mouth pursed with distaste and Rachel nodded sympathetically.

'Horrible for you, I'm sure. Now, I'd just like to listen to your chest, if you wouldn't mind.' She waited while Miss Parish unbuttoned her coat then listened to her chest. 'And I'll take your temperature too,' she told her once she had finished doing that.

Miss Parish sat perfectly still while Rachel checked her temperature. The reading was higher than it should have been and Rachel nodded because it confirmed her suspicions. Sitting down at her desk again, she smiled at the old lady.

'It looks as though you have bronchitis, Miss Parish. The symptoms you described certainly point towards it—wheezing, shortness of breath, a persistent cough that produces considerable quantities of phlegm. Your temperature is higher than it should be, too, which is another indication.'

'Bronchitis? Well, I never!' Miss Parish looked shocked.

'It's an acute form and we can treat it quite easily with a course of antibiotics,' Rachel said soothingly. She wrote out a script and handed it over along with detailed instructions aimed at making the old lady more comfortable in the interim.

Miss Parish listened attentively to what she said then nodded. 'I shall follow your advice, Dr Mackenzie. Thank you. I must say that I was very sorry to hear what had happened to your son. It can't be easy for him, having his wedding cancelled like that.'

'I'm sure Ross will deal with it,' Rachel replied evenly, hoping to avoid any further well-meaning comments.

'Oh, I'm sure he will. Once he gets over

the shock, I expect he'll realise that it's better it happened now rather than later.' Miss Parish stood up. 'So many young couples end up getting divorced these days and that must be just as distressing for them, I imagine.'

Rachel frowned as the old lady bade her goodbye and left. Would the marriage have ended in divorce if it had gone ahead? she wondered. A couple of days ago she would have pooh-poohed the idea but she was no longer so sure. Heather obviously had had her doubts and that was why she had called the wedding off.

She sighed because it just proved how difficult relationships really were. Even those that seemed guaranteed to succeed could and did fail. It took both love and an awful lot of commitment to build a lasting relationship, not to mention that vital spark Matt had mentioned. That was essential too. Thinking about Matt immediately reminded her of what had troubled her all weekend and she groaned. She didn't want to go down that road again!

She buzzed in her next patient, a young woman with a screaming toddler suffering from a nasty ear infection. It was hard to make herself heard over the din the poor little mite was making but Rachel was glad because it blotted out any other thoughts. She didn't want to dwell on what a special relationship Matt must have had with his late wife when it was so painful, didn't want to sit here daydreaming about him when she had work to do. It wasn't the best way to get things back onto a normal footing, which was what she desperately needed to do.

Lunchtime arrived and Rachel hurried to Ross's room to see how he had fared. She caught him as he was about to leave and her heart ached with motherly concern when she saw how drawn he looked. Having his wedding cancelled at the eleventh hour must have been a terrible experience for him despite the brave front he was putting up. She wasn't sure that he should be at work, but he was adamant that he wanted to be there when she broached the subject.

They chatted for a couple of minutes, but her heart was heavy as she watched him leave. No matter what Ross claimed, she knew he must be devastated by what had happened. A tear trickled down her cheek and before she could wipe it away, Matt appeared. He took one look at her and gently steered her along the corridor into his room.

'Is it Ross?' he asked as he sat her down in a chair and offered her the box of tissues off his desk.

'How did you guess?' Rachel blew her nose

and tried to get a grip on herself. The situation was difficult for Matt too and she didn't want to upset him as well.

'Simple deduction, Watson. If you eliminate everything else, whatever you're left with, no matter how improbable it seems, must be the solution.'

Despite herself Rachel laughed. 'Is that a fact, Sherlock?'

'It certainly is, Doctor.' Matt smiled back her at her and her heart immediately lifted. She couldn't deny that she was touched that he should try to cheer her up when he must be feeling extremely low himself.

'So how is Ross holding up?' he asked, placing the box of tissues back on the desk.

'Fine, according to him.' She shrugged when he looked quizzically at her. 'You know Ross. He isn't one to wear his heart on his sleeve. He was the same when he was a child, very self-contained and serious…a little too serious, in fact.'

'Did he have much contact with his father while he was growing up?' Matt asked quietly, and Rachel tried to hide her surprise. It was the first time he had ever asked her a personal question like that in all the time they had worked together and she couldn't help wondering what had prompted it that day.

'None at all,' she replied, determined that she wasn't going to make too much of his sudden interest. Maybe he wanted to find out more about the past in the hope it would provide a clue as to how to bring Ross and Heather back together? If that was the case then she was all for it. She would do anything at all to see Ross happy again.

'Ross's father made it clear from the outset that he wasn't interested in him,' she explained truthfully. 'I don't blame him in a way because he was only eighteen when Ross was born. Not many boys of that age are ready to become fathers.'

'You were very young to be a mother but you coped,' Matt pointed out, and she sighed.

'Yes, I know, although I wouldn't have managed nearly as well if my parents hadn't supported me. They were marvellous.'

'It must have been hard, though, even with their help.' Matt's tone was gruff and she frowned when she heard it. She couldn't help wondering why he sounded so uptight all of a sudden, apart from the obvious reason, of course. He must miss Heather dreadfully and the thought made her heart ache for him.

'It wasn't easy. Finding the time to study and look after Ross was a real juggle. Looking back, I don't know how I fitted everything in.' She gave a little laugh, hoping it would lighten the sombre mood. 'If I had to do it now, I'd need a few more hours tagged onto the end of each day!'

'I imagine you fitted it all in by dint of sheer

hard work. You should be proud of yourself for what you've achieved, Rachel.'

'I am extremely proud of Ross, although I can't claim any credit for how he's turned out,' she said firmly. 'Ross put in the effort himself.'

'I don't just mean raising Ross but what you've achieved.' Matt leant forward and she could see the light in his eyes, a hint of fire she hadn't noticed before and certainly hadn't expected. Her heart gave a little bounce then started to race as he continued.

'You must have worked incredibly hard to get through medical school. I remember how difficult it was to keep up with all the work and when you factor in a child as well…' He shrugged. 'Not many people could have done what you've done, Rachel.'

'I always dreamed of being a doctor,' she said quietly, deeply moved by the compliment. To know that Matt admired her made all the years of hard work and struggle seem even more worthwhile.

'And you achieved your dream. You're a damned fine doctor. Your patients couldn't speak more highly of you.'

'Thank you. It means a lot to hear you say that,' she murmured, feeling a little choked with emotion.

'It's nothing more than the truth. You should be proud of yourself. You've achieved everything you set out to do.'

Had she? she wondered. Had she really achieved every single dream she'd ever had? Just days ago Rachel would have agreed with him but she was no longer sure if it was true. Once upon a time she'd had other dreams for the future. She had buried them as deeply as she could over the years because there'd been no time to worry about them, but they were still there, maybe not as bright and as shiny as they had been, but still there.

Her heart caught as she looked at Matt and remembered all the hopes she'd had at one time for a happy marriage like her parents', a loving relationship that would sustain her throughout the years. She had abandoned those dreams because she'd been afraid of what would happen if she allowed herself to fall in love again. She had done it once, fallen in love with Ross's father, and it had been a disaster... Hadn't it?

The thought pulled her up short. Having Ross hadn't been a disaster, far from it. It had been a turning point. Knowing she'd had a child to provide for had given her the impetus she had needed, pushed her to make a good life for herself and her son. Without Ross, she might not have studied as hard, but made another mistake and fallen in love with someone else who might have held her back.

Rachel took a deep breath as she faced the

facts, head on. Her life could have turned out very differently if she hadn't had her son. For one thing, she might never have met Matt.

Matt decided to stay on after evening surgery ended. He wanted to make a start on that report Ambulance Control had requested while the facts were fresh in his mind. After all, it wasn't as though there was anything to rush home for, was there?

His heart sank at the thought of returning to an empty house, although he knew that he would have to get used to it. With Heather gone he would be spending a lot of time on his own. He had just drafted out a rough time-table of events when there was a tap on his door and Rachel came into the room.

'I spotted your light was still on as I was passing,' she explained, coming over to the desk. She frowned when she saw the timetable he had made. 'Is that about the accident?'

'Yes. I thought I'd better make a start on that report.'

Matt glanced at the notes he had written, trying not to think about the fact that Rachel lived on her own as well. It had no relevance to his situation, especially as it was obviously her choice to do so. By no stretch of the imagination could he believe that she hadn't had lots of offers to change her single status.

'Do you need any help?'

Matt barely heard what she said. Not once in the all the time they had worked together had he wondered why Rachel was single, but now the question clamoured for his attention. She was a beautiful and highly intelligent woman and there must be lots of men keen to share their lives with her, so why had she resisted? Was it because she had never met anyone she had cared enough about to spend her life with?

Thoughts whizzed around inside his head.

It was only when he realised that Rachel was waiting for him to answer that he pulled himself together. 'It's kind of you to offer, but I don't expect you to give up your evening as well, Rachel.'

'It's not a big deal, Matt.' She gave a little shrug. 'And it isn't as though I've anything better to do. In fact, I'd be glad to help, if I'm honest. It will stop me worrying about Ross if I have something else to think about.'

'In that case, I'd be glad of your help. Thank you.'

Matt smiled up at her, feeling warmth ripple along his veins when she smiled back. She pulled up a chair and sat down beside him, leaning over so she could read what he had written. Matt felt his whole body grow tense when he inhaled her perfume but he was wise to the effect it could have after that morning and quickly brought himself under control. So long as he focussed on what he was doing, there shouldn't be a problem.

With Rachel's help they soon compiled a list of events and the times they had occurred. Anything hazy—such as what Ross and Gemma, their practice nurse, had been doing before they had arrived—they marked with an asterisk so they could check it later. By eight o'clock they had the bare bones of the report prepared and Matt was delighted they had accomplished so much.

'Excellent!' he said, leaning back in his chair and easing the crick out of his neck. 'I thought it would take a lot longer than that.'

'Two heads, et cetera,' Rachel replied with a grin, and he laughed.

'Too right, especially when the two heads are in tune with one another.' Matt smiled back, feeling more relaxed than he had felt in days. Ever since Heather had told him that she was leaving Dalverston, it had felt as though his nerves had been strung out on a rack. However, after just an hour of working with Rachel he felt much better, so much better, in fact, that he was reluctant to let the evening end there.

'How do you fancy going out for dinner?' he suggested impulsively. 'I don't know about you but all this extra work has given me an appetite. I could eat a horse!'

'I'm not sure if you'll find horse on the menu anywhere in Dalverston,' she replied lightly, although he saw a hint of colour run up her cheeks.

Did she think he was being presumptuous by asking her out? he wondered, then immediately dismissed the idea. Of course Rachel didn't think that. They were colleagues and having dinner together wasn't anything to get worked up about.

'Hmm, good point. I'll have to settle for a steak instead.' He pushed back his chair, not wanting it to appear as though he was pressurising her to go out with him. It was her decision and he would abide by whatever she decided to do, although he really hoped she would say yes.

It was unsettling to realise just how much he wanted her to agree and he hurried on. 'So long as it comes with all the trimmings, I'll be more than happy.'

'I have to confess that I'm hungry too,' she admitted, standing up. 'I can't remember when I last had a decent meal—it must have been last week. I definitely didn't cook anything for myself over the weekend.'

'Me neither,' Matt agreed, sliding the notes they had made into a folder. 'The most I've managed is tea and toast for the past couple of days. My poor stomach must think my throat's been cut.'

She laughed as she headed for the door. 'It sounds as though we're both in desperate need of some proper sustenance. How about that new place on the bypass? I believe they do excellent steaks there.'

'Sounds good to me.'

Matt managed to hide his delight as he switched off the light and followed her along the corridor. It was just dinner with a colleague, he reminded himself, although he had to admit that it felt somewhat different to the usual staff outings he had attended in the past. For one thing, he and Rachel would be by themselves tonight and that was something that didn't usually happen. Even when they had spent all that time planning the wedding, they hadn't been on their own—Ross and Heather had been with them. This would be a whole new experience for them.

He took a steadying breath as he stopped beside the reception desk, determined that he wasn't going to let himself get carried away by the thought. 'I'll set the alarm and follow you out. We can go in my car, if you like. That way you can have a glass of wine with your meal without worrying about driving home.'

'Thanks, but it's easier if we take both our cars. It will save all the hassle in the morning of getting here.'

It was on the tip of Matt's tongue to tell her that he would give her a lift, but he sensed that would be overstepping the mark. 'Fine. I'll see you there, then.'

He waited until she had left then switched the phone through to their on-call service and set the alarm. There was only his car left in the car park when he went outside and he hurried over to it, shivering as a blast of icy wind blew down from the hills. The temperature had dropped over the weekend and it looked as though they were in for a really cold spell. Still, it wouldn't be long before he got to the restaurant and warmed up, he consoled himself.

He started the engine, smiling at the thought of meeting Rachel there. Maybe it was only dinner with a colleague but it was good to know that he wouldn't be spending the rest of the evening on his own. Was that her main attraction? he wondered suddenly. Was he so eager for her company because he was lonely?

He tested out the theory and discovered that it did fit. However, deep down he knew it was more than that. Loneliness didn't explain the way he had responded to her recently, did it?

CHAPTER FOUR

RACHEL could feel butterflies flitting around her stomach as she entered the restaurant. It wasn't very busy with it being a Monday evening and she had no trouble getting a table. She told the waiter that she was expecting someone to join her and sat down to wait, trying to control the frantic fluttering inside her. It was just dinner with Matt, nothing more, nothing less, and definitely nothing to get worked up about.

Matt arrived a few minutes later, looking big and imposing as he stopped to speak to the waiter. Rachel noticed several women glance his way and look a second time too as

he made his way over to her. No wonder, she
thought as he took off his coat and draped it
over the back of a chair. He was an extremely
handsome man and she wouldn't blame any
woman for finding him attractive.

'This is nice.' He looked around the restaurant with obvious pleasure. 'It all looks very
sleek and modern without being too stark and
bare. Call me old-fashioned but I like a bit of
clutter around the place.'

'Me too, probably too much clutter,' she
agreed ruefully.

'So you don't go in for the minimalist
look that Ross favours?' Matt queried,
loosening his tie. He undid the top button of
his shirt as well and Rachel hurriedly
averted her eyes when she felt those pesky
butterflies start flapping even more wildly.
She had seen Matt wearing a variety of
outfits over the years they'd worked
together, from the jeans he had worn on

staff outings to the suits he preferred for work, so why was she reacting this way to a glimpse of bare tanned flesh?

'No, it's not my taste at all. As for Ross, well, he probably favours that style because it's the complete opposite from what he grew up with.'

Rachel hurriedly dismissed the question. They were there to have dinner, not so she could analyse how she felt about Matt. He was a colleague and a friend, and that was all she needed to know.

'Really?' Matt sat back in his chair, obviously keen to hear more, and she continued, finding it easier to talk about such a safe topic.

'We lived with my parents for a long time, you see, so Ross grew up in a house decorated according to his grandparents' tastes. Mum is very much into chintz and frills and I think that's why Ross rebelled and opted for something very different when he bought his own home.'

'It must have been a help to have your parents on hand,' Matt said quietly, and she nodded.

'Oh, it was. Mum not only looked after Ross while I was studying but while I was doing my rotations as well. I don't know how I'd have managed otherwise. The hours a newly qualified doctor has to work are horrendous.'

'I remember how exhausting it was working such long shifts. My first post was as a junior house officer in A and E at a hospital in London—I don't think I went to bed for three days solid at one point because I was on call.'

'Thank heavens they've put a stop to young doctors working such terrible hours, although it's no picnic for them even now,' she agreed. 'It's madness to expect someone to function properly when they're exhausted.'

'It is. I certainly couldn't have coped with looking after Heather on top of the hours I worked. Thankfully, I didn't need to because

Claire took care of all that. She gave up work when Heather was born so she could be a full-time mum.' Matt sighed. 'You've not had an easy time, Rachel, have you? You didn't have that option.'

'It wasn't that bad,' she protested, touched by the concern in his voice. 'As I said, Mum and Dad were marvellous and once I'd completed my GP training, life became much easier. It was still hard work, of course, but at least I didn't need to work such gruellingly long hours.'

'When did you move out of your parents' house?' Matt asked curiously.

'When Ross was about twelve. I was earning a decent salary by then and I was able to afford a mortgage. Mum still helped out if I needed a hand, but it was good to be independent at last.'

'You value your independence, then?' he said quietly, and she frowned when she caught a hint of something she couldn't identify in his tone.

'Yes, I suppose I do. It was a long time before I was able to strike out on my own and it's important to me to know that I'm not beholden to anyone.'

'Is that why you've never married?' He shrugged when she looked at him in surprise. 'It just seems strange that you're still single. It certainly can't be for lack of offers.'

Rachel felt the colour rush to her cheeks and stared down at the table. Had she imagined that sensuous note in Matt's voice, that hint of sexual attraction? She must have done because there was no sign of it on his face when she looked up.

'I guess I've never met anyone I wanted to spend my life with,' she said lightly, opting for a partial truth.

The waiter arrived just then to take their order and by the time they decided what they wanted, the moment had passed. However, several times during the evening Rachel found herself wondering if she should have been more up front with Matt and explained that she had been wary of falling in love in case she had committed another error of judgement. For some reason she couldn't explain it seemed important that he should know the truth. How odd.

They left the restaurant shortly after ten p.m. Matt would have happily stayed there longer but it was obvious the staff were waiting to close for the night. If anything the temperature had dropped even further and he saw Rachel shiver as they walked towards their cars.

'Brr, it's freezing,' she declared, huddling into the collar of her coat. 'Do you think it will snow tonight?'

'It could do, although it's probably a bit too cold at the moment.' Matt carried on past his car and saw her look at him in surprise. 'I'll just make sure you get off safely,' he explained, and she laughed.

'Ever the gentleman even in the freezing cold!' She quickly zapped the locks open and turned to him. 'I enjoyed tonight, Matt. Thank you. Next time, it's my treat.'

'I'll hold you to that,' he said, aiming for lightness and hoping he had succeeded. The thought of them spending another evening together was so enticing that he had a sudden urge to grin but managed to restrain himself. There was no point scaring her into thinking she'd had dinner with a lunatic!

'You do that.'

Before he could say anything else she reached up on tiptoe and kissed him on the cheek. Her lips were cold from the wind and Matt sucked in his breath when he felt them touch his skin. It was just one of those kisses that people exchanged all the time, he told himself firmly, a social nicety, nothing to get steamed up about, but he wasn't convinced. He could call it whatever he liked, but it was still a kiss and his body appreciated that fact even if his brain insisted on trying to rationalise it.

Desire flooded through him, bringing about a very predictable response, or at least one that would have been predictable several years ago. The fact that it hadn't happened in so long he could barely remember the last time made his heart almost stutter to a stop.

Rachel gave him a quick smile as she stepped back. 'I'll see you tomorrow, then. Take care going home. There could be ice on the roads.'

'I…um…you too,' Matt said numbly as she got into her car and closed the door. He waited while she backed out of the parking space, even managed to wave as she drove away, but every action was an effort when his body was clamouring for something it hadn't experienced since Claire had died.

He walked back to his car and got in then sat there, letting the feelings pour through him. This had gone beyond what he had felt at the weekend, way beyond that first tentative awakening of desire. What he was feeling now was something more earthy, more powerful, more urgent. He wanted to make love to Rachel and enjoy every inch of her delectable body, and then enjoy *her* enjoying *him*. Maybe it was the passage of time but he couldn't remember feeling this need so intensely before, not even for Claire.

The thought shook him to the core. His love for Claire had been the mainstay of his life, the one thing that had never been in doubt. Surely he wasn't doubting it now just because he wanted to have sex with another woman?

Matt knew he needed to work out what was going on and that he couldn't do it there. He needed to go home and think about it, calmly, rationally. He drove himself home, keeping his speed well below the limit because he was aware that his reactions weren't as sharp as they should have been. As soon as he got in, he made himself a cup of coffee and took it into the sitting room. There in the room he and Claire had spent so many happy evenings, he let himself remember their life together, all the good times they'd had, the fun, the laughter, the love.

Tears welled to his eyes but he didn't try to stop them falling. He had spent years being strong for his daughter's sake and it was time he allowed himself an outlet for his emotions. He had loved Claire so much, would have loved her for ever more, but she had died and left him on his own. He needed to cry for the woman he had lost and he also needed to cry for himself too.

Rachel drove home carefully, heeding her own advice. Although the main roads had been gritted, she could see a shimmer of frost on the tarmac when she turned into the lane leading to her cottage. She negotiated the bends with extra care and drew up with a sigh of relief. Thank heavens that was over.

Stepping out of the car, she went to hurry up the path and shrieked in alarm when her feet suddenly skidded from under her. She landed with an almighty thud, wincing as her right knee took the brunt of her fall. Getting to her feet again wasn't easy when her knee felt as though it was on fire but she needed to get inside. She certainly couldn't spend the night outdoors in weather as cold as this.

She hobbled up the path and let herself in. It seemed an awful long way to the kitchen but a cold compress should help to prevent her knee swelling up. By leaning against the wall and hopping, she finally made it to the kitchen and dug a bag of frozen peas out of the freezer, wrapping it in a tea-towel before applying it to her knee. There was already a huge bruise forming and she guessed that the whole knee would be black and blue by the morning.

She sighed as she held the makeshift compress against her swollen joint. What a miserable end to a lovely evening. Maybe it was payback for that kiss? She hadn't planned on it happening—it had been purely an impulse. She wouldn't have given it a second thought normally either. However, the moment her lips had connected with Matt's cheek, she had realised her mistake. Social kissing may be all well and good, but not when the person she was kissing was Matt, apparently.

Her breath caught as she remembered the warmth of his skin against her lips. She touched a finger to her mouth and shuddered when she felt an echo of that heat still lingering there. It was hard to believe the brief contact could have left such a lasting impression. Had it made the same impression on Matt, though?

Common sense insisted that the answer to that question should be a resounding no but she found it difficult to accept it. There had been several occasions recently when he had looked at her with an awareness in his eyes that she hadn't seen there before. Even the interest he had shown tonight when he'd asked her why she had chosen to remain single was a new departure for him and she couldn't help wondering what had changed. Was it possible that Matt no longer saw her simply as a colleague?

The thought made her heart race even though she had no proof that it was true. Rachel sighed as she put the now-soggy bag of peas back into the freezer and lifted out a bag of sprouts. All she knew for certain was that *her* feelings towards Matt had altered recently and altered dramatically too. She would have to be extra careful around him and make sure that she didn't let him know how confused she felt. And that meant no more kissing for *any* reason!

Matt was getting showered the following morning when the telephone rang. Snatching a towel off the rack, he hurried into his bedroom and picked up the receiver. Surprisingly, after all the emotional upheaval of the previous evening, he had slept soundly. It was as though a weight had been lifted from his shoulders, making him see that he had needed an outlet for his feelings for a very long time.

'Matthew Thompson.'

'Matt, it's me, Rachel. I'm sorry to phone you so early but I need a favour.'

Matt felt a rush of heat invade him and sank down onto the bed. Hearing Rachel's voice reminded him vividly of the dreams he'd had during the night, dreams of such an explicit nature that his body immediately quickened as he recalled them. It was an effort to respond calmly when every cell was suddenly on the alert.

'Of course. What can I do for you, Rachel?'

'Can you give me a lift into work? I very stupidly slipped on some ice last night as I got out of my car and hurt my knee. It's not serious,' she added hurriedly, 'but I don't think I can actually drive myself there today.'

'Do you want me to run you to hospital so you can have it X-rayed?' Matt suggested in concern.

'Thanks, but there's no need. I'm sure there's no serious damage—it's just badly swollen. It should be back to normal in a couple of days' time.'

'Are you sure you should be going into work?' he protested. 'The best thing for it is rest and you won't be able to do that if you're having to jump up and down, attending to patients.'

'I'll manage,' she assured him. 'I've spent the night with a bag of frozen peas strapped to it and that's helped.'

Matt chuckled. 'It's good to know the professionals opt for the same remedies as their patients. Frozen peas indeed!'

Rachel laughed. 'It was either peas or sprouts, and the sprouts were far too lumpy, I discovered. They kept rolling about!'

Her laughter rippled down the line and Matt felt his senses spin all over again. Why had he never realised before what a gorgeously sexy laugh she had? It was an effort to concentrate as she continued.

'I'll be ready any time you say, so when should I expect you?'

He glanced at the bedside clock. 'Will half an hour suit you?'

'Fine. I'll be able to hobble around and

make myself some breakfast before you get here. Everything seems to take twice as long as normal when you have a gammy leg.'

She said goodbye and Matt went back to the bathroom. However, the thought of her struggling as she tried to make herself something to eat didn't sit well with him. His conscience simply wouldn't allow him to let her soldier on on her own.

It took him a scant ten minutes to get himself dressed and drive the short distance to Rachel's house, and instead of ringing the front doorbell he went straight round to the back. It would save her having to trek down the hall if he used the rear entrance, he reasoned. He tapped on the door, feeling his heart lurch when she opened it. Rachel in the flesh was every bit as beautiful and as sexy as she had appeared in his dreams.

'You're early!' she exclaimed.

'I thought you could use some help.' He

smiled at her, determined to get a grip on such wayward thoughts. 'I'm a dab hand at making tea and toast for the injured.'

'Oh, that's really kind of you, Matt. Thank you.' She hobbled over to a chair and sank gratefully down onto it. 'I hadn't realised how difficult it is to do even simplest tasks like filling the kettle when you need to hang onto something to stay upright.'

'Well, I'm here now so you just sit there and rest that leg.' He glanced at her bruised knee and grimaced. 'That's a real beauty. You really need to raise it to reduce the swelling— here, use this chair.'

He pulled over a chair and gently manoeuvred her leg until it was resting comfortably on the cushion. Rachel groaned, the lines of strain easing from her beautiful face.

'That feels *so* much better.'

'Good.'

He turned away, although he could have

happily stood there all day and simply enjoyed looking at her. He set to work instead, scrambling some eggs and making a stack of toast as well as a pot of tea to go with them. Rachel nodded approvingly as he placed everything on the table and sat down.

'This looks delicious. Scrambled eggs are my absolute favourite.'

'We aim to please.' Matt helped himself to a slice of toast, thoroughly enjoying the experience of sharing breakfast with her. He could get used to seeing Rachel across the breakfast table each morning, he decided, very used to it indeed. The thought was so highly inappropriate when he was trying to be sensible that he immediately chased it from his mind and applied himself to his meal.

Rachel scraped the last morsel of eggs off her plate and sighed in contentment. 'My compliments to the chef. That tasted every bit as good as it looked.'

'Thank you kindly.' Matt smiled at her, loving the way her eyes sparkled with golden glints when she was feeling happy. It was something else he hadn't noticed before and he added it to the ever-expanding list. 'Although I have to warn you that my repertoire isn't exactly extensive. I can roast a chicken, grill chops, scramble eggs and that's about it.'

'Better than a lot of men, I imagine,' she said cheerfully, attempting to stand up.

'Whoa!' Matt put out a restraining hand and eased her back down onto the chair. 'Where do you think you're going?'

'I was only going to stack the dishes in the machine,' she protested.

'I'll do that.' He picked up their plates and took them over to the dishwasher, adding the rest of the crockery as well as the pan he had used for the eggs.

'Thank you.' Rachel glared at her knee in frustration. 'It's a real nuisance not being able to do things for myself. I only hope the swelling goes down soon.'

'It will probably take a couple of days before you get your full mobility back and even then you'll need to be careful,' he warned her. 'If you try doing too much too soon, you'll only make matters worse.'

'In other words, I need to be patient.' She grimaced. 'The worst part was last night. The stairs here are really steep and I had a devil of a job getting up them to go to bed. And I had to come down on my bottom this morning—not a pretty sight, believe me!'

Matt laughed at the wry note in her voice although he couldn't help feeling concerned. If there was an emergency, Rachel would have great difficulty getting out of the cottage. 'Maybe you should sleep downstairs until your knee is better.'

'I would do but the bathroom's upstairs, so I have to go up to get to it.' She gave a little shrug as she lifted her leg off the cushion and cautiously stood up. 'Not to worry. I'll soon be back to normal.'

Matt doubted it but he decided not to say so. He waited while she found her coat and bag then offered her his arm so she could lean on him while they went out to his car. It was obvious from the strain on her face that it was an effort for her to walk even that short distance but he knew it was pointless advising her to stay at home and rest. She was far too dedicated to go off sick unless she really couldn't avoid it, and in all truth they would find it very difficult to manage without her when they were trying to lighten Ross's workload.

It was frustrating not to be able to do more to help her, though. Matt resolved to keep an eye on her and make sure she didn't push herself too hard until her knee was better. What Rachel needed at the moment was someone to take care of her and he was more than happy to take on that role. The fact that he wouldn't mind it being a long-term project flashed through his mind but he didn't dwell on it. It was too soon for ideas like that, way too soon.

CHAPTER FIVE

MORNING surgery was exceptionally busy that day. There was a nasty tummy bug doing the rounds and a lot of people wanted to see the doctor. Rachel dispensed sympathy and advice in almost equal measures. Although this type of winter vomiting bug was very upsetting for the victims, so long as they behaved sensibly by restricting their food intake and maintaining their fluid levels, it was rarely life-threatening. The only exceptions were the elderly and the infirm, and young babies and infants. They needed extra care so she was particularly concerned when one young teen-age mum brought in her three-month-old son.

'How long has Charlie been like this, Melanie?' she asked, studying the poor little mite. Little Charlie's lips looked extremely dry and when she gently opened his mouth and checked, his tongue was dry to the touch too, worrying signs in a child this young.

'Since yesterday lunchtime. He was sick after he'd had his bottle and kept being sick all afternoon long. He also had the most horrible nappies,' Melanie added, her nose wrinkling in disgust.

Rachel stifled a sigh. It wasn't the girl's fault that she lacked experience and hadn't realised just how urgent the situation was. 'Has Charlie had anything to drink since then, cool boiled water, for instance?'

'No. The health visitor told me to give him some the other week, but he doesn't like it,' Melanie explained. 'He prefers his milk.'

'I see.' Rachel gently pressed her index finger against the baby's arm and was unsurprised to find that his skin was lacking in elasticity. Charlie was exhibiting all the classic signs of being severely dehydrated and he needed urgent treatment. Picking up the phone, she dialled the emergency services and requested an ambulance, briefly outlining the problem to the operator when she was connected. Melanie looked at her in dismay after Rachel hung up.

'An ambulance! But surely Charlie isn't so ill that he needs to go to the hospital?'

'I'm afraid he is, Melanie,' Rachel replied quietly. 'He's extremely dehydrated and it's very dangerous in a baby this young. He needs to be rehydrated as quickly as possible so he'll be put on an intravenous drip when you reach the hospital.'

'But I thought you'd just give me some medicine to stop him being sick,' Melanie wailed, tears pouring down her face.

'I wish it was that simple.' Rachel struggled to her feet and hobbled around the desk. She placed a comforting arm around the young mother's shoulders. 'The doctor at the hospital will also do a blood test to check Charlie's fluid and salt levels. Once an infant becomes severely dehydrated, it's essential to ensure that the right balance is maintained.'

'I wish I'd known all this before,' Melanie sniffed. 'I'd have brought Charlie in to see you last night if I'd thought he was in any danger.'

'Do you have anyone to help you with him?' Rachel asked and Melanie shook her head.

'No. I was brought up in care. I don't know where my parents are—they never came to visit me while I was in the children's home. And as for Charlie's dad, well, he didn't want to know when I told him I was pregnant.'

'I see.' It was an all too familiar tale and Rachel's heart went out to her. She had been so fortunate to have her parents there to help her through the first difficult years following Ross's birth, she thought.

There wasn't time to dwell on it then, however. The ambulance had arrived so she saw Melanie and baby Charlie out to Reception then went back to her room. However, as she worked through her list, Rachel decided that something needed to be done to help other young mums like Melanie. If they had somewhere they could go for advice it could prevent another situation like this from occurring.

She decided to mention it to Matt and see what he thought about the idea. If they put their heads together, she was confident that they could come up with some sort of a plan. A smile curved her mouth. It may mean extra work for her but working with Matt was always a pleasure and never a chore.

Matt went straight to Rachel's room after his last patient left. He had found himself clock-watching, willing the time to pass so he could check up on her. She was sitting at her desk, her head bowed as she jotted down some notes on a pad.

Matt felt a rush of heat erupt in the centre of his chest. She had no idea he was there so he could study her at his leisure and he made the most of the opportunity. Her hair was a riot of rich chestnut curls as it tumbled around her face. It looked so silky and so soft that once again he was struck by the urge to touch it. Then there was her skin, so smooth and satiny that he ached to touch that too. Everything about her was appealing, seductive, and he couldn't understand why he had never realised it before. Had he been walking around with his eyes closed for the past few years? Or had he been afraid to notice how beautiful she was because of what it could mean? By admitting that he was attracted to her, it meant that he was getting over Claire.

The thought shook him. He had never considered the idea that he had been deliberately clinging on to the past but it was true. He had been afraid to let it go when he had been scared of what the future held. Until Claire had died his life had been mapped out and mapped out in a way he had wanted it to be. He'd had a job he loved, a child he adored and a happy marriage. However, Claire's untimely death had changed everything. He had been cast adrift, his future sent spinning out of his control, and the only way he had been able to cope had been through clinging onto what he'd had—especially his love for Claire.

Deep down he knew it wasn't enough any longer. He needed more than just his memories. But having more meant taking risks and he couldn't imagine placing himself in the position of getting hurt. Even supposing he found someone else to love, did he have the courage to risk his heart again?

Thoughts tumbled around his head and Matt realised that he needed time to deal with his inner turmoil. He quietly backed out of the room but just as that moment Rachel looked up and saw him. Her face broke into a smile and his heart clenched in fear. Even now it might be too late. He already felt far more for Rachel than he should have done.

'Ah, just the person I wanted to see.' Rachel smiled at Matt across the desk, her mind still busy with the plans she had made for the new teenage pregnancy advisory service she was hoping to set up. She glanced at her notes again and nodded. Yes, it was do-able. Just.

She looked up, eager to share her ideas with him, and frowned when she realised that he hadn't moved an inch. He was still standing in the doorway, looking to all intents and purposes as though he wished he was anywhere but there. What on earth was wrong with him?

'Are you all right, Matt?' she began, but he didn't let her finish.

'I'm sorry, Rachel, but I can't stop right now. I've an urgent call to go to. I'll catch up with you later. OK?'

'I…um…yes, of course,' she murmured, although he couldn't possibly have heard her seeing as he had already left.

Rachel grimaced as she struggled to her feet. It must be something really important if Matt couldn't spare even a couple of minutes to talk to her. She gathered up her case notes and made her way to the office. Carol leapt up from her desk when she saw Rachel coming in and rushed over to the door.

'You should have buzzed me,' the receptionist admonished her. 'I'd have come and got those notes off you. Here, sit yourself down and take the weight off that knee.'

'Thanks.' Rachel gratefully subsided onto a chair. 'I never realised before just how long that corridor is,' she joked, easing her leg onto a handy cardboard box full of stationery.

'And it'll feel even longer by the end of the day,' Carol retorted, taking the cushion off her chair and placing it under Rachel's swollen knee. 'You should be at home, resting, instead of galloping around this place.'

'I'm not sure galloping is the right way to describe it. More like a hop, skip and hobble. All I need is a parrot on my shoulder and I could double for Long John Silver!'

Carol laughed. 'At least you can see the funny side, that's something.'

'That's probably all,' Rachel replied pithily. She looked round when Ross poked his head round the door, putting up her hand when she saw his expression change as he spotted her injured leg. She had managed to avoid telling him what had happened by going straight to her room when she had arrived that morning. However, there was no way she could avoid it any longer. 'There's no need to panic, darling. I just slipped and bumped my knee getting out of the car last night. It looks far worse than it is.'

'Why on earth didn't you phone me, Mum?' He came into the room and crouched down in front of her, shaking his head when he saw the bruising. 'I'd have come straight round.'

'I know you would but I didn't want to bother you. Anyway, there was no need for you to come haring round,' she added, deliberately distorting the truth a little. The last thing Ross needed at the moment was to have to worry about her. 'Matt sorted me out. He even came round to make breakfast for me this morning *and* drove me to work.'

'Oh, right. I see. Well, that was good of him but you still should have phoned me and let me know.'

Rachel breathed a sigh of relief when Ross accepted her explanation at face value. He wasn't to know that she had struggled on by herself the previous night, neither did she intend him to know. She smiled at him, her heart aching when she saw the shadows in his eyes. There was no doubt at all that recent events had taken their toll on him, despite his attempts to carry on as normal. 'I feel suitably rebuked. I'm sorry, darling.'

'I'll let you off this time so long as it doesn't happen again,' he told her with mock severity, and she laughed. He gave her a peck on the cheek and straightened up. 'Have you got that list of calls ready, Carol?' he asked, turning to the receptionist.

'Here it is. There's nothing urgent. Most folk seem to be suffering from that wretched tummy bug.'

Carol handed over the list of house calls that needed doing along with a printout of the relevant case notes, and Rachel frowned. Nothing urgent? But what about the call that Matt had gone rushing off to? She waited until Ross had left before broaching the subject.

'Matt mentioned something about an urgent call. Who's he gone to see?'

'Matt?' Carol looked blankly at her. 'Sorry, I don't know what you mean. Ross is on call today, not Matt, and there's been nothing urgent, as I said.'

'My mistake. I must have got the wrong end of the stick. Blame it on the painkillers.'

Rachel passed it off although she couldn't help feeling puzzled. Matt had been very clear about being called out, so what on earth was going on? If he needed to go somewhere then why not say so…? Unless it had had something to do with Heather and he hadn't wanted her to know.

Rachel sighed sadly. She had never known Matt to prevaricate before and it was upsetting to know that he felt he needed to do so now. She must make it clear to him that she had no intention of taking sides when it came to their respective children. She certainly didn't want it to have a detrimental effect on their relationship—whatever that relationship was nowadays.

Once again the uncertainty caused a rush of panic. Mere days ago she had been happy to call Matt her friend but friend wasn't enough any longer, neither was colleague. Matt seemed to have assumed a new role in her life, one that demanded a great deal of her attention, too.

How did he view her? she wondered, harking back to the question that had troubled her the previous night. Was she still just the same person he had worked with all these years or did he now see her differently too?

One part of her preferred the security of thinking that nothing had changed so far as

Matt was concerned while another part knew that it had. The trouble was that she had no idea if it made the situation easier or more complicated. It all depended on *how* Matt felt about her and only time would tell her that.

Matt drove round for almost an hour before he went back to the surgery. By then his initial panic had subsided and had been replaced by a definite feeling of embarrassment. What on earth had he been thinking, rushing off like that after only the flimsiest excuse? he thought grimly as he parked his car. Rachel only needed to check with Carol and she would soon discover that there'd been no emergency and then he would have some explaining to do.

His mouth compressed as he pushed open the surgery door and went inside. He wasn't used to making a fool of himself and he didn't enjoy the experience. From now on he had to stop acting like an idiot and behave like the rational and responsible person he was.

'Matt, hi!'

Rachel's voice brought him to an abrupt halt. He turned slowly around, steeling himself for the questions and the answers as well. How the hell was he going to explain his abrupt departure if she asked him outright where he had been? He may have resorted to a small white lie before but he couldn't lie to her again. He would have to tell her the truth, yet the truth was so terrifying that he didn't dare to imagine her reaction. Could he really see himself confessing that he was attracted to her and that was why he had made such a rapid exit?

'If you have a few minutes to spare any time this afternoon, can we get together? There's something I want to discuss with you.'

She hobbled unsteadily over to the desk and Matt immediately forgot about himself as he grasped hold of her arm. 'You need to sit down and rest that leg. Come on, let's get you back to your room before you do yourself any further damage.'

He held onto her arm as they made their way along the corridor. Rachel sank down onto her chair with a groan of relief that spoke volumes and he shook his head. 'You need to slow down, Rachel, instead of rushing about the place.'

'If only I could rush.'

She smiled up at him, her eyes filled with amusement and just the tiniest smidgen of concern. Matt knew without a word being exchanged that she had found out that he hadn't been to see a patient, only she was too polite to say so. The thought made him feel guiltier than ever as he sat down on the edge of the desk.

'Well, whatever speed you're moving at it's too fast for you. If you need someone to fetch and carry for you then ask, Rachel. That's all it takes.'

'I know, and thank you.' She looked up at him so trustingly that he knew he had to confess, although how he should go about it was another matter entirely.

'About before, when I went rushing off,' he began, but she held up her hand.

'You don't have to explain, Matt. I understand.'

'You do?' He could barely hide his dismay and she sighed softly.

'Yes. You didn't want to upset me, but it's all right. Really it is. I'm not going to take sides. They have to work this out themselves.'

'They do?' Matt murmured, because he had no idea what she was talking about.

'Yes.' She leant forward and he could see the sympathy in her eyes. 'If Heather has contacted you then it's only natural that you should want to see her. I promise I won't say a word to Ross. For one thing I don't intend to interfere and for another I don't want to raise his hopes unnecessarily.'

'Oh. Right. I see.' Matt didn't know what to do. He knew that he should explain that Heather hadn't contacted him but that meant opening up a whole new can of worms. He mentally argued with himself about the rights and wrongs of keeping quiet but still hadn't decided when Rachel changed the subject.

'If you've got a few minutes to spare now, can we talk about this idea I've had?'

She launched into her proposal for a teenage pregnancy advisory service and he didn't interrupt her. Maybe it was cowardly to take the easy way out but it was a lot less stressful for both of them. Admitting that he was attracted to her would alter the dynamics of their relationship and he wasn't sure if it was a good idea. What it all boiled down to was one simple question: was he willing to risk losing Rachel as a friend when he wasn't sure if he was ready for any other kind of a relationship?

CHAPTER SIX

'I KNOW it will mean extra work for us all, but after what happened today with Melanie and baby Charlie, I honestly feel that it would be worth it. If we can prevent another near-tragedy from happening, it has to be a good thing, don't you agree?'

Rachel waited for Matt to answer, hoping that he would see the benefits of her proposal. She hadn't realised how passionately she felt about the idea until she had explained it to him. Now she could only hope that he would share her enthusiasm.

'I think it makes an awful lot of sense,' he said slowly. 'Yes, it will entail extra work, especially while we set everything up, but the flip side is that we may not get so many callouts or visits to the surgery. Once the younger mums gain more confidence, they will be less likely to call us in unnecessarily.'

'Exactly!' Rachel beamed at him, delighted that he had taken her ideas on board. Not that Matt had a closed mind when it came to any new ventures; he was always open to fresh ideas that would benefit their patients. It was one of the things she had always admired about him, his willingness to listen and learn, but there again there were so many other things to admire that it was hard to select just one from the whole delicious package.

She cleared her throat, aware how easily her mind could run off at a tangent if she let it. 'There may be funding available too. I'll need to check on that. But if we could get some sort of a grant, we could buy in extra help as and when it's needed—a midwife to speak to the mums before they give birth, maybe a health visitor or even one of the more experienced mothers to offer practical day-to-day advice—that type of thing. I know some of those services are available already but I get the impression that the younger mums in particular don't feel there is enough help on offer to them.'

'I get the same impression. In fact, one of my patients mentioned only the other day that all the new mums get nowadays by way of guidance are three one-hour sessions before their babies are born. They're supposed to cover everything during that time from the birth right through to the end of the baby's first year.'

'Is that all?' Rachel exclaimed. 'It definitely isn't enough, especially not for the very young mums like Melanie. They need a lot more support than that to prepare them for motherhood.'

'They do. I imagine you're particularly keen to help them because of your own experiences,' Matt suggested quietly.

'You're right, I am. I know what it's like to feel out of your depth, even though I was one of the lucky ones and had my parents to help me.'

'Then if you feel so strongly about it, Rachel, we'll see about setting it up as soon as possible.' He glanced at his watch and grimaced. 'Now I'm afraid I'll have to cut and run. It's my turn for the antenatal clinic so maybe we can continue this discussion later. There's still a lot of ground we need to cover.'

Rachel checked her desk diary and shook her head. 'I won't be able to fit it in today, I'm afraid. I've got the anti-smoking clinic this afternoon so I'll be tied up until evening surgery begins. That clinic always seems to run over time for some reason.'

'How about tonight, then?' Matt stood up

to leave. 'If we hope to secure sufficient funding for this scheme to go ahead, we need to work the costs into next year's budget. The figures are due in at the end of January so we'll have to get a move on.'

'If you're sure you don't mind,' she began hesitantly, not wanting him to suspect how much the idea appealed to her. Spending another evening with him was something she hadn't anticipated and her heart was kicking up a storm at the prospect.

'Of course I don't mind.' He gave her a quick grin. 'Let's do it the civilised way and talk it all through over dinner.'

'That would be lovely,' she agreed, and he nodded.

'Good. It's a date.'

He straight left after that but it was a couple of minutes before Rachel followed him from the room. It had been a turn of phrase, that was all, she told herself firmly as she made her way to the meeting room where the anti-smoking clinic was being held. It certainly wasn't a date and she had to get that idea right out of her head. They were just two colleagues who planned on having dinner together while they discussed work-related issues. Yet even though she understood that she couldn't help wishing that he had invited her out for a very different reason. To know that Matt wanted to spend some time with *her* would have meant a great deal.

The afternoon flew past and before Matt knew it, it was time for evening surgery. He saw his first half dozen patients without encountering any major problems. Most people had come with the usual complaints that were the mainstay of any busy general practice—coughs and colds, ear infections and aching joints. He treated everyone the same, taking the time to listen to them and affording them the courtesy they deserved. He liked people and wouldn't have chosen to do this job if he didn't care.

His next patient was a teenage boy called Adam Shaw. He came shuffling into the room, looking very ill at ease. Matt asked him to sit down and smiled encouragingly at him. 'So what can I do for you today, Adam?'

'I…well…um…' Adam turned bright red with embarrassment. It was obviously an ordeal for him to explain the reason why he had come.

'There's no need to be embarrassed, Adam. I assure you that I won't be shocked by whatever you tell me.' Matt looked the boy firmly in the eyes. 'Just spit it out and tell me what's wrong.'

'It's down here, you see,' Adam muttered, pointing to his groin. 'There's something… well, not right.'

'In what way?' Matt's tone was businesslike because he knew it was the fastest way to extract the information he needed. At this rate they would still be sitting here at midnight!

That reminded him of what he had planned for the evening but he managed to brush the thought aside. If he started thinking about Rachel and this dinner they were having, he would be in no better state than young Adam.

'Can you describe your symptoms for me, Adam?'

'I…um…I've had this sort of *discharge*,' Adam explained, his face turning even more fiery. 'And everything feels sort of *swollen*, you know.'

'I see. Right, I'll need to examine you so if you could just pop behind the screen and remove your trousers etcetera, I'll be with you in a moment.'

Matt gave the boy a couple of minutes to get ready then examined him. Adam's testicles were indeed swollen and he admitted that he experienced discomfort every time he passed urine. Add that to what the boy had told him about there being a discharge and Matt was soon able to make a diagnosis.

'It looks as though you have non-specific urethritis, Adam,' he told the teenager once they were sitting down again. 'The urethra has become inflamed and that's why you have these symptoms. My main concern now is to identify the micro-organism that has caused it, although most cases of NSU are due to a sexually transmitted disease like chlamydia. If that is the cause in this instance it means I shall have to contact all your sexual partners and check if they require treatment too.'

'Oh, no! I can't believe this is happening.' Adam put his head in his hands and groaned. 'Will you have to tell my parents? They'll go mad if they find out!'

'No.' Matt shook his head. 'You're seventeen so there is no need to involve anyone apart from the girls you've slept with. It's imperative that they are checked out too because if it is chlamydia, it can have serious repercussions for them in the future. For you as well as it can cause infertility if it isn't treated.'

'I've only slept with one girl and that's the truth, Dr Thompson. It was my first time and I thought it was hers, too, but apparently not.'

Adam was obviously deeply upset by the idea that he had been misled. Matt gave Adam a moment to collect himself then carried on, wanting to get all the information he needed. He made a note of the girl's name and address then collected some samples to send to the lab for testing. He then wrote out a script for erythromycin and told Adam to come back to see him in a week's time when the lab results would be back. He would explain then that Adam would need to make follow-up visits for the next three months to make sure he hadn't suffered a relapse.

He made a note to check if Adam's girlfriend was a patient at the practice and buzzed in his next appointment, glancing at the clock as he did so. Just half an hour to go until surgery ended and he and Rachel could enjoy that dinner they had planned. Maybe it was only a working dinner but that didn't matter. Being with her was enough, probably more than he should allow himself given his parlous state of mind. However, he was only flesh and blood and he couldn't help wanting to spend time with her even if he wasn't sure if it was wise.

Rachel made a quick trip to the bathroom as soon as her last patient had left. If she'd had any idea that she would be going out that night she would have worn something more glamorous than the sober grey suit she had put on that morning. There wasn't much she could do about it now, so she washed her face, applied a fresh coat of lipstick and fluffed up her hair, wishing as she did every day that it would lie smoothly around her face instead of insisting on curling so riotously. Still, it was thick and glossy and that was something in its favour even if it refused to be tamed.

She went back to her room and was just attempting to struggle into her coat when Matt appeared. He looked so big and handsome as he came striding into the room that her heart gave a girlish leap of delight. She could just imagine him striding across the deck of a pirate ship, or riding hell for leather across an open plain. He was real hero material from the top of his dark hair to the tips of his well-shod feet, she decided dreamily.

'Need a hand with that?'

He took the coat from her and slid it up her arms before she could blink, and she shivered when she felt his hands smoothing the collar into place. Even though there were several layers of clothing between his hands and her flesh, she could feel her skin tingling, tiny flurries of heat that scorched along her veins and made it difficult to think. It was only when he removed his hands that she was able to pull herself together and she sighed softly. She needed to keep her emotions under far tighter control if she wasn't to make a fool of herself tonight.

'Thanks. I just need to get my bag then I'm ready to leave,' she told him, determined not to get sidetracked again. She bent over to open the bottom drawer of the desk, quite forgetting about her injured knee, and gasped when it suddenly gave way beneath her.

'Careful!' Matt grabbed hold of her arm and steadied her. He shook his head. 'What did I say before about you asking for help, Rachel? Leave it. I'll get it.' Bending down, he retrieved the bag, grimacing when he discovered how heavy it was. 'What on earth do you keep in this thing? It weighs a ton.'

'Oh, just the usual things,' she replied, making a mental note to be more careful in future. She was trying to remain on even keel and that wouldn't be possible if at every turn Matt ended up touching her. Her heart lurched as she recalled the strength of his grasp as he had set her safely back on her feet and she hurried on. 'The problem is that I never seem to get round to clearing out the clutter and just keep adding to it.'

'You women and your handbags,' Matt declared, rolling his eyes as she limped around the desk.

'Look who's talking,' she retorted, glancing pointedly at his case. 'You don't exactly travel light yourself, do you?'

'Ah, but the difference is that all I keep in here are essentials—pills and potions, etcetera.' He tucked her hand into the crook of his arm as naturally as though it had been part of their daily routine for ever and laughed, mercifully covering the tiny gasp that escaped her when she found herself pressed against the solid length of his body.

'And that's it? You're willing to swear on oath that you don't keep anything else in there?' she retorted, doing her best to keep her emotions firmly leashed.

'Of course,' he declared loftily, pausing in the doorway to switch off the lights. 'Everything this case contains is work-related.'

They headed along the corridor at a snail's pace, Matt adjusting his speed to accommodate the fact that she couldn't hurry. Whilst Rachel appreciated his thoughtfulness it didn't help one little bit. Each slow, deliberate stride he took brought his hip and thigh into even closer contact with hers and it was the sweetest kind of torment imaginable. Even though she was wearing heavy winter clothing, she could feel the power and strength of his body as clearly as though they had both been naked.

Heat rushed through at the picture that instantly sprang to her mind and she bit her lip. The situation was going from bad to worse and she had no idea what to do about it. All she did know was that she mustn't let Matt suspect how she felt or it could ruin everything. She would rather have him as a friend and a colleague than not have him in her life at all.

They went to the same restaurant they had been to the previous night. Matt had suggested going somewhere different for a change but Rachel had claimed that she wasn't dressed for anywhere too upmarket. To his mind she looked fine, more than fine, wonderful, in fact, although he forbore to say so. This was a working dinner, he reminded himself as the waiter showed them to their table. It wasn't a date.

The thought of what a real date might have entailed shimmered in front of his eyes like a mirage. *If* they had been out on a date, he'd have been able to tell Rachel how he felt, admit that he was attracted to her, maybe even confess his fears about getting hurt. And after dinner was over they might even have decided to continue the evening. It wasn't as though they didn't know one another, so it wouldn't have felt as though he was rushing her if he'd invited her back to his house. They could have sat by the fire in the sitting room and drunk coffee, and then he would have kissed her, slowly, deeply, passionately.

His body tingled as he imagined how sweet her lips would taste, like honeyed nectar. He would kiss her once then kiss her again and keep on kissing her until it was no longer enough for either of them. Even though

Rachel had never chosen to have a long-term relationship, he knew that she would be a passionate and responsive lover, a tender and giving lover too. It was her nature to be generous and there would be no holding back. She would give herself to him with all the generosity of the person she was and he would bury himself in her softness, her sweetness, and allow it to heal him. He would become whole again in her arms, fearless and unafraid of the future. The thought was almost too tempting to resist.

'I'm going to have the same as I had last night.'

Rachel closed her menu and placed it on the table. Matt's head whirled as he struggled to separate the mirage from what was actually happening. 'Good idea. I think I will too.'

He placed his menu on top of hers, forcing out the images that crowded his head. Rachel deserved to be loved and cherished, nothing less, and he wasn't sure yet if he could do that. 'So have you had any more thoughts about this new advisory service?' he asked to distract himself from that strangely unsettling thought.

'Just one. I was wondering if we should offer contraceptive advice as well.' Rachel paused as though she hadn't made up her mind about the benefits of such a service and Matt nodded encouragingly. He wanted to fill his head with as many new ideas as possible in the hope they would shut out everything else.

'It would make a lot of sense. Dalverston has never had a proper family planning clinic and, in my opinion, it's a huge oversight. Admittedly, the number of unplanned pregnancies in the town is relatively low compared to some other places, but they still happen. Kids need to understand that they have to behave responsibly, and not just to avoid getting pregnant either.'

'STDs, you mean?' Rachel queried.

'Yes. I had a young man in tonight who's a prime example of the value of such a service. It looks very much as though he's caught some sort of sexually transmitted disease—probably chlamydia—and it was the first time he had slept with a girl too. Youngsters like him need to understand that they can't afford to take any chances whether it's their first time or their hundredth.'

'I agree, although I suppose that must sound rather hypocritical.'

'Hypocritical?' He frowned. 'What do you mean?'

'That I'm hardly a shining example of how to behave sensibly seeing as I was a teenage mum myself,' she explained wryly.

'That's just plain silly, Rachel. All right, so you didn't plan on having Ross, but everyone is allowed to make one mistake in their lives.'

'Thank you. And I have to confess that I wouldn't change things even if I could.

Having Ross was the best thing that ever happened to me. I know I worked twice as hard as I would have done if I hadn't had to support him.'

'There you go, then. You've nothing to feel bad about. In fact, I can't think of a better role model for the kids than you.'

Matt heard the husky note in his voice and picked up his glass of water, hoping that Rachel wouldn't thank him for the compliment. If she did he might be tempted to hand out a few more and that would be the wrong thing to do. He had to remember that he wasn't in a position to court her.

The incongruity of the old-fashioned term should have made him laugh, yet it was the best way to describe how he felt. He wanted to *court* her, to woo her and charm her into liking him. He tried to remember if he had felt the same way when he had met Claire but it was too long ago to recall his feelings. His love for

Claire had been both rich and fulfilling, but it had changed over the years they'd been married. Their passion had mellowed, the urgency they had felt in the beginning turning into a closeness that had sustained them both. But all of a sudden he knew that if he fell in love with Rachel it wouldn't be the same. It couldn't be. He couldn't imagine the passion he felt for her growing weaker with time.

Matt's breath caught as he was forced to acknowledge the truth. Loving Rachel would be a very different experience from loving Claire. Admitting it seemed like the ultimate betrayal.

CHAPTER SEVEN

RACHEL sensed a certain undercurrent bubbling away while they ate. It wasn't anything Matt said, but a feeling she had that something was troubling him. To all intents and purposes he behaved exactly the same as normal but she was too sensitive when it came to him to miss even the smallest signs. The thought unsettled her so that when he suggested having coffee after their meal, she refused. It seemed wiser to bring the evening to an end rather than prolong it.

They left the restaurant a short time later and walked over to where they had parked the car. There was a thick layer of frost on the windscreen and once Matt had settled her in the passenger seat, he got out a can of de-icer and set to work. Rachel huddled deeper into her coat, although it wasn't the chill of the night that was making her feel so cold but the worry of it all. Had Matt sensed something amiss from her own behaviour, perhaps?

'Let's get this heater going.' Matt got into the car, bringing with him a blast of icy air. He frowned when he saw her shiver. 'You're frozen solid! I should have turned on the engine instead of leaving you sitting here.'

He sounded genuinely upset and she couldn't bear to hear him berate himself when she was the one at fault. She had to get over this ridiculous crush and set everything back on a normal footing.

'I'll live,' she said lightly, making a deter-mined effort to sound upbeat. 'I'll have you know that I'm a lot tougher than I look!'

'Oh, I don't doubt it.' He grinned at her. 'I

bet you tear up telephone directories with your bare hands for fun, don't you?'

'You'd better believe it!' Rachel flexed her fingers and laughed, feeling easier now that their usual harmony had been restored. Maybe she had been reading too much into the situation, she thought, glancing at Matt as he drove them out of the car park. He'd probably been concentrating on the pros and cons of this new venture, making sure that it would be worth all the extra work involved. She had rather sprung it on him and maybe she should have given him more time to weigh it all up.

'Look, Matt, if you have any reservations about this proposal of mine, please, say so. I know how stretched we are and offering a new service like this is bound to stretch us even more.' She shrugged. 'I don't want to cause problems for everyone, believe me.'

'You aren't. As we agreed earlier it could end up saving us a lot of time. Add in the very real benefits to both the mums and their babies and it has to be a good idea. No, I can honestly say that I don't have any reservations at all. It's an excellent idea.'

'Oh, right. Good. I'm glad you feel like that.'

There was no doubt in her mind that he meant what he said and Rachel let the subject drop. They passed through the town centre and headed towards the outskirts of the town. Matt drew up at the side of the road when they reached the lane where she lived and turned to her.

'I know you'll think I'm fussing, Rachel, but are you sure you can manage tonight with that knee? I'd hate to think of you taking a tumble down those stairs of yours.'

'I won't,' Rachel replied, swivelling sideways so she could look at him. Her breath caught when she saw the concern in his eyes but she refused to allow herself to get carried away. Matt was just being his usual kind and thoughtful self. She held up her hand as though swearing an oath. 'I promise on my honour that I shall be extra careful what I do. Does that set your mind at rest?'

'A bit, but I'd feel better if you would stay at my house tonight.' He hurried on, obviously keen to forestall any objections she might make. 'And before you say anything, you won't be putting me out. Just the opposite, in fact. You'll be doing me a favour.'

'A favour?' she repeated numbly, struggling to get her head round the idea.

'Mmm. I won't get a wink of sleep if I'm worrying about you falling down those wretched stairs.' He smiled at her, a smile of such tenderness that her heart immediately melted. Could he have looked at her that way if he didn't genuinely care? she wondered giddily. The thought was so mind-blowing that it was hard to concentrate when he continued.

'You can have the bedroom in the annexe.

It's en suite so there's no stairs to negotiate if you need to use the loo during the night. There's even a little fold-down seat in the shower which should make life easier for you, shouldn't it?'

'I…er…I suppose so,' Rachel murmured, hoping to gain herself a little time. She groaned because even if she'd had a couple of hours to decide, it wouldn't have made the decision any easier. It wasn't the safety factor she was worried about, or at least not where it concerned her knee. It was the thought of spending the night under Matt's roof that was giving her hot and cold chills. That was far more dangerous.

'It's the ideal place for you to stay while your knee heals. You'll be able to potter about and not do yourself any more damage.' He leant over and squeezed her hand. 'Say you'll stay, Rachel, even if it's only for tonight. Please. Just for me.'

* * *

'There's clean sheets on the bed and fresh towels in the bathroom. Heather often invited one of her friends to stay over so the place is always ready for guests.'

Matt stepped aside so that Rachel could see into the small but functional bathroom. Everywhere gleamed brightly, the black and white tiles sparkling in the light, and she nodded, battening down the urge to laugh. Matt was acting like a hotelier, pointing out the room's good points, and she was acting like a guest. How ridiculous was that?

She went back into the bedroom, taking stock of the quilted throw on the king-sized bed, the comfy chair positioned next to the dressing table. It was an attractive room and she knew she would be comfortable sleeping there, but was she mad to have agreed? Surely she was making a difficult situation worse by sleeping in Matt's home even if she wasn't actually sleeping with *him*.

Heat rushed up her cheeks and she busied herself with removing her coat to hide her embarrassment. Matt must have seen her struggling because he immediately stepped forward to help. He slid the coat off her shoulders and it was all she could do to hide her shiver when she felt his hand brush against the side of her neck. Even though it was only the briefest of contacts she felt it register in every cell of her body like a surge of electricity. She heard Matt draw in a ragged breath and glanced round in surprise, wondering if he had felt it too, but he was already moving away.

'How about a cup of tea?' he suggested, hanging her coat in the wardrobe.

'That would be lovely. Thank you.'

Rachel waited until he had left then sank down on the bed. She must stop wondering if Matt felt the same way as she did or this night would turn into a disaster. Unbuttoning her jacket, she laid it on the quilt then smoothed down the front of her blouse. It was warm in the house and what with that plus her own inner thermostat going haywire, it felt as though she was burning up. Somehow, she had to remain calm no matter what happened.

Once again her temperature spiked as a whole raft of possibilities flooded her mind. They ranged from the innocuous—Matt giving her a goodnight peck on the cheek—to the preposterous—a night of unbridled passion—and she moaned. What a time for her imagination to run riot!

'Tea's ready,' Matt shouted, and she struggled to her feet. Tea and some undemanding conversation were just what she needed to calm her nerves.

She made her way along the hall and found Matt coming out of the kitchen, carrying a tray. He smiled as he nodded towards the sitting room.

'We may as well drink it in here. It's more comfortable.'

He led the way, placing the tray on a table before going over to the window to draw the curtains. He'd already lit the fire and the logs were starting to spit as they caught light. Rachel sat down in one of the squashy arm-chairs, sighing with pleasure as she looked around the room.

'This is such a lovely room, Matt. It always feels so welcoming.'

'I've always loved it,' he agreed, passing her one of the cups before sitting down on the sofa. 'I suppose that's the main reason why I haven't redecorated it for years. I like it just the way it is, although I'm going to have to buy a new sofa at some point. There's more sag than bounce in these cushions, I'm afraid.'

Rachel laughed at his wry expression. 'It looks fine to me, but there again my own sofa isn't exactly in its first flush of youth.'

'Obviously a woman after my own heart. You like to get full value out of your furniture too.'

He returned her smile, mercifully missing the start she gave. Of course she wasn't after his heart, she told herself sternly. That was ridiculous. She took a sip of her tea then looked up when the phone suddenly rang. Matt frowned as he got up to answer it.

'I wonder who that can be at this time of the night.'

Rachel watched as he crossed the room and picked up the receiver. He had his back to her and she found herself studying the strong, straight line of his spine. Everything about him was solid and dependable, she thought, both inside and out. He possessed the rare gift of making people feel that no matter what mishap befell them, he would help them sort it out. It was one of his major strengths as a GP and it was also one of the things that appealed to her most. Matt was someone she could turn to in a crisis and he would never let her down. She had never thought that about any man before.

'No, please don't apologise. I quite understand why you're worried, Mrs Morris. Leave it with me. I should be there in about ten minutes' time.'

Rachel frowned when she heard what he had said. 'What's happened?'

'That was Mrs Morris from Prescott Lane on the phone. One of her boys is running a temperature and he also has a strange rash on his legs.'

'Has she phoned the on-call service?' Rachel asked.

'Yes, over an hour ago, apparently, but nobody's turned up yet and that's why she phoned me.' Matt's tone was grim. 'There's been two cases of meningitis in the area recently so I appreciate why she's so worried.

We can't afford to take any chances that this might be another one.'

'Certainly not,' Rachel agreed. 'Are you going over there now?'

'Yes. I know the on-call service should cover it but that isn't the point. The boy needs to be seen sooner rather than later.' He headed to the door then paused and glanced back. 'I don't know how long I'll be so don't wait up for me, Rachel. I'll see you in the morning.'

'Of course. Be careful, though, Matt. The roads are very icy tonight. You don't want to have an accident.'

'Don't worry, I shall be extremely careful. We can't afford to have two of us hobbling around the surgery, can we?'

He smiled at her and just for a second his face was unguarded. Rachel's breath caught but before she could react, he swung round and a moment later she heard the front door slam. She struggled to her feet and made it to the window in time to watch him drive away. Resting her forehead against the glass, she tried to recall the expression on his face. Had she imagined it, seen what she had wanted to see? She wasn't sure, but for a moment there'd seemed to be such hunger in his eyes as he had looked at her, such need, that just thinking about it made her shiver.

She sighed as she stared out at the darkness. Even if Matt did feel something for her there was no reason to believe that he would do anything about it.

'The good news is that I'm ninety-nine percent certain that Robbie doesn't have meningitis.'

Matt sympathised when he heard the boy's parents gasp in relief. As a parent himself, he understood how worried they must have been. He smiled at them, trying not to think about all the other worrying issues he had to contend with at the moment.

'Whilst Robbie undoubtedly has a fever and a rash, there's nothing else that points towards it being meningitis. There's no neck stiffness, no sign of photophobia—that's an aversion to light—no headache or sickness.'

He pressed a glass tumbler against the blotches on the boy's legs, blanking out all thoughts of what had happened before he'd left the house. The desire he'd felt for Rachel had almost overwhelmed him. If he hadn't made such a rapid exit he would have had the devil of a job to contain it. The thought was enough to make his heart race.

'As you can see, the rash disappears when you press the glass against it. That doesn't happen with the meningitis rash.'

'So you think it's some sort of a virus?' Robbie's father queried.

'It could be.' Matt turned to the boy, his gut instinct telling him to probe a bit more deeply. 'Is there anything else that you haven't mentioned, Robbie? Something that's happened which you haven't told your mum and dad about?'

Robbie bit his lip, looking so sheepish that Matt knew he was right. He sat down on the edge of the bed and said firmly, 'Nobody is going to tell you off if you've done something silly, son. We just want to find out what's making you feel so ill.'

'It was the rat,' Robbie muttered, glancing warily at his parents.

'A pet rat?' Matt said, shaking his head. Mrs Morris opened her mouth to speak. He didn't want any interruptions now that Robbie had got this far.

'No, just a rat down by the river. Me and my friends were playing there the other day and we found this rats' nest, you see. We weren't going to hurt them,' Robbie said quickly. 'We just wanted to have a look at them. We got a stick and poked around a bit, but then one of them bit me on the ankle. Just here. See.'

'That looks nasty,' Matt said as the boy rolled down his sock and showed him his ankle. The area surrounding the bite was badly inflamed, pointing towards it being infected. 'It would definitely explain why the lymph nodes in your groin are swollen. The infection has spread throughout your body. No wonder you've been feeling so poorly.'

'But rats carry the plague, don't they, Doctor?' Mrs Morris put in fearfully. 'I saw a programme on the television a few months ago and they said that the plague started because the country was overrun with rats!'

'Usually it's the fleas off the rats that bite people and pass on the plague,' Matt explained patiently. 'Thankfully, we don't have that problem in this country any more, although there are other diseases that rats can carry. That's why anyone who's bitten by a rat should always seek medical attention as soon as possible.' He glanced at the boy. 'Robbie is probably suffering from rat-bite fever and the good news is that we can clear it up with antibiotics. However, no more poking about in rats' nests, young man. Steer well clear in future.'

'I will.'

Robbie lay down, looking very sorry for himself. Matt wrote out a script for penicillin once he'd made sure the boy wasn't allergic to it. He handed it to the parents along with a couple of sachets of the medicine which he happened to have in his case. At least Robbie wouldn't need to wait until the morning when the prescription was filled before he started on the medication.

'Thank you, Dr Thompson,' Mrs Morris said gratefully. 'And thank you for coming out as well. We're really grateful, aren't we, love?'

'We are indeed,' her husband agreed.

'I'm only sorry that you had to wait so long,' Matt told them as they saw him out. 'I don't know what went wrong tonight but I'll get onto our on-call service and make sure it doesn't happen again.'

'Should I phone them and let them know we don't need a doctor to call now?' Mr Morris queried.

Matt shook his head. 'There's no need. I'll do it.'

He went out to his car and put through a call to the on-call service. He explained that there was no longer any need for a doctor to visit the family then asked why there had been such a delay sending someone out. He sighed when he was briskly informed that it was due to a combination of the number of calls they had received and staff shortages. He hated to think that their patients might not be getting the service they deserved.

He drove home, making good time until he reached the outskirts of the town where a heavy layer of frost on the tarmac made him slow down. As he had told Rachel earlier, the practice couldn't afford to have two of them injured. Thinking about Rachel immediately set loose a whole host of emotions. The temptation to go and see her when he got in was very strong, but he had to resist it. He simply couldn't trust himself to be around her at the moment and not do something silly, although maybe it would be all right if he just made sure that she had everything she needed. It would take only a moment and he could retire to his bed, duty done.

Matt grimaced as he drew up outside the front door. He knew that he was merely looking for an excuse to see her, but admitting it wasn't enough to deter him. He went straight to the annexe, pausing outside the door while he mustered his composure. The last thing he wanted was to make Rachel feel that he was coming onto her.

CHAPTER EIGHT

RACHEL was about to switch off the bedside lamp when she heard Matt's car turning into the drive. She hesitated, undecided what to do. Although he had told her not to wait up, she was tempted to go and see how he had got on. She sighed when she heard the front door open. Interested though she may be in their patients' welfare, it wasn't the real reason she wanted to see him, was it?

She reached for the switch but before she could turn off the lamp, there was a knock on the door. Rachel froze. Although a moment ago she had been longing to see him, the thought of seeing him now was suddenly giving her hot and cold chills. How could she hope to carry on a conversation when she was in this frame of mind?

'Rachel, are you awake?' His voice carried softly through the door and she knew that she had to answer. Matt must have seen that her light was on as he drove up and it would look very strange if she didn't reply.

'Yes, I'm awake,' she croaked, groaning when she realised how strained her voice sounded. Matt would soon realise there was something wrong if she carried on like this. 'Come in,' she called firmly.

'I spotted your light was still on,' he explained as he came into the room. 'I thought I'd better check that you have everything you need.'

'Yes, thank you.' Rachel returned his smile, hoping he couldn't tell how on edge she felt. This was a whole new territory for her because she'd never entertained him in her bedroom before.

Nerves assailed her once more but fortunately he didn't appear to notice her discomfort. Walking over to the window, he drew the curtains tightly together. 'We may as well keep out any draughts. It's bitterly cold out tonight. I wouldn't be surprised if the temperature drops below freezing point.'

'It's been heading that way for the past few days,' she agreed, although the state of the weather was the least of her problems. All night long she had kept returning to that moment before Matt had left but she still hadn't decided if she'd been right to think that he had wanted her and the uncertainty of not knowing was the worse thing of all. If she knew how he felt then she might know what to do about it.

The thought made her heart lurch and she hurried on. 'So how did you get on? Was it another case of meningitis?'

'No, I'm glad to say.' He came over to the bed. 'It turns out that young Robbie managed to get himself bitten by a rat and has rat bite fever. A course of antibiotics will soon sort it out.'

'Well, that's good news. I'm sure his parents must be relieved.'

'Oh, they are. I'm only sorry they had to wait so long for a doctor to turn up and set their minds at rest.'

'Did you phone the on-call service to find out why there'd been a delay?'

'I did. Sheer number of calls, apparently, plus they have a couple of their staff off sick.'

'That wretched bug, no doubt,' she said ruefully, and he nodded.

'I expect so, although it's not really good enough, is it? Patients shouldn't have to wait so long for help to arrive. I was always uneasy about employing an on-call service before we signed up to it and this proves I was right to have my doubts.'

'But we've never had a problem before,' she protested.

'Maybe not, but that's no excuse. Our patients deserve a reliable service every single day of the year and it's up to me to make sure they receive it.'

'That's ridiculous, Matt! It's not your fault that they happen to be short-staffed when it's a particularly busy night.' Rachel could tell that he wasn't convinced and leant forward, determined to make him see sense. 'You can't blame yourself for what happened tonight.'

'No, but I intend to keep a closer eye on what's happening from now on.' He shrugged. 'It's only by the grace of God that it wasn't another case of meningitis we were dealing with.'

He turned away but she caught hold of his hand. 'Just because there was a glitch tonight, it doesn't mean it will happen again,' she countered, trying to ignore the tingles that were spreading up her arm. Matt's hand felt so big and warm that she was loath to release it even though she knew that she should. 'They're a reliable firm and you have to trust them to get on with the job.'

'Yes, ma'am!' Matt said smartly. He eased his hand out from hers, making a great production of flexing his fingers, and Rachel laughed.

'If you're trying to make me feel bad about crushing your hand, forget it. There's no way that I hurt you. I mean, look at the size of your hand compared to mine.'

Rachel laid her hand, palm up, on the quilt, feeling her heart jolt when Matt laid his on top of it. His hand was so much larger than hers that it completely engulfed it. She could feel the roughness of his palm against the smoothness of hers, the strength of his fingers, and shuddered. It had been a long time since a man had touched her like this, a long time since she had wanted this kind of contact either.

Her eyes rose to his face and her breath

caught when she saw the expression it held. There was an awareness there that she understood only too well, but it was tinged with something else, something that made her blood heat. All of a sudden she knew that she hadn't imagined what had happened before. Matt had wanted her then and he wanted her now, wanted her in every way a man could want a woman. Finally seeing the proof of that broke down the barriers she had erected around herself to guard against making any mistakes.

She reached up towards him but he was already bending down to her so that they met halfway. Rachel felt heat envelop her when their mouths met and she gasped, heard him gasp as well. The kiss could have lasted no longer than a second but she was trembling when they drew apart and could see that Matt was trembling too. Maybe they hadn't planned on this happening but it was what they both desperately needed.

Matt looked at her for a long moment, his eyes grazing over her face before they came to rest on her mouth. 'If you want me to stop, you only have to say so,' he said, his voice grating in the quiet of the room.

Rachel took a quick little breath but her own voice sounded equally ragged when it emerged. 'I don't want you to stop, though. Really I don't.'

He was reaching for her before she had finished speaking but she didn't care. When he sat down on the bed and drew her into his arms, she went willingly, letting the soft curves of her body nestle against the hard contours of his. He held her close against him while he trailed fiery little kisses over her eyes, her nose, the line of her jaw, so that she was dizzy with need by the time he claimed her mouth again.

Rachel clung to him as she kissed him back, making no attempt to hide the hunger she felt. She wanted this so much, wanted Matt to kiss her, hold her, make love to her. When his hands went to the buttons on the borrowed pyjamas she wore, she helped him, working them free until the top fell open. She heard him take a shuddering breath as his hands went to the edges of the fabric. She could tell that he was struggling for control as he parted the jacket, and shivered. That Matt should want her this much was more than she had dared hope for.

'You're beautiful, Rachel, so very, very beautiful.'

His tone was reverent as he studied her lush curves. When he reached out and gently cupped her breasts in the palms of his hands, she closed her eyes and gave herself up to the sensations that were flooding through her. She had made love before but not once had she felt this way, filled with passion, over-whelmed by need. Making love with Matt was very different to anything she had experienced before.

He stroked and caressed her breasts until she could barely contain the desire that was building inside her. When he bent and placed his mouth over her nipple, she cried out. He drew back, his eyes intent as he searched her face and what he saw there obviously reassured him because he bent and kissed her other breast, drawing the rigid nipple into his mouth and suckling her.

Rachel gasped as a rush of desire flowed through her. Burying her fingers in his hair, she held his head against her, whimpering softly as he continued to lavish attention on her breasts before letting his mouth glide down her body. He kissed her waist, encircling her ribs with nibbling little kisses that made her twist and writhe with unbearable pleasure. Then when his tongue found her navel and dipped in and out, she groaned.

Nothing had prepared her for how Matt made her feel.

His mouth retraced its route, stopping frequently to scatter more kisses over her body until Rachel could barely think. When he drew back and stood up, she could only murmur in protest, but he shook his head.

'I'm not going anywhere, Rachel. Not unless you tell me to.'

'I don't want you to go,' she said huskily.

'Good.' He dropped another deliciously sexy kiss on her mouth then stripped off her pyjama pants and his own clothes as well. Rachel just had a moment to marvel at the power and beauty of his aroused body before he lay down beside her and took her in his arms, holding her so close that she could feel his erection pressing against her.

'You can still say no, Rachel,' he whispered, his breath warm and sweet on her cheek. 'If this isn't what you want, we can stop right now.'

'It is what I want, though.' She looked deep into his eyes so there would be no mistake. 'I already told you that, Matt, and I meant it.'

'It's what I want as well.'

His voice throbbed with need and she shuddered when she heard the hunger it held. Opening her arms, she welcomed him into her embrace, her body suffused with desire when he entered her in one swift, breath-taking thrust. They made love with a desperation that spoke volumes, then made love a second time with a pure unbridled joy that brought tears to both their eyes.

Rachel knew that she had never shared this kind of closeness with anyone before and never would. It was only with Matt that she felt secure enough to give herself so completely, to shed all the restraints and allow herself to feel each and every emotion. She trusted Matt and that made all the difference. For the first time in her life she felt safe, secure, wanted, although she shied away from the one word that would have made the experience perfect. Until she knew how Matt truly felt, she couldn't claim that she felt loved.

Day came slowly, the darkness gradually fading as dawn crept in. Matt was already awake and had been awake for hours. He had been too keyed up to sleep and had spent the night listening to the sound of Rachel's breathing as she had lain beside him. Now, as he studied the delicate beauty of her profile, he was assailed by doubts. Had he made a mistake by sleeping with her?

Last night he had been caught up in the throes of a kind of madness, his body demanding the release that only making love to her could give him. Now he'd had time to think and panic was setting in. He may have sated his hunger but at what cost? He would never forgive himself if he hurt Rachel, yet he was aware of how easy it would be to do so. After all, what could he offer her? One night of passion wasn't enough, but he wasn't able to offer her anything more. Not yet.

He rolled onto his back, feeling the emotions welling up inside him. Guilt and joy, sadness and elation were all mixed up together so that it was hard to know how he really felt. Had he betrayed Claire's memory by making love to another woman?

Guilt swamped him even though his head rejected the idea, insisted that he had nothing to feel guilty about, that it was time he moved on and lived his life in the present instead of the past. However, it wasn't the only issue, was it? There was Heather—how would she feel if she found out? Would she be upset that he had slept with another woman, especially when that woman was Ross's mother? He knew that Heather liked Rachel but that wasn't the point. By sleeping with Rachel, he may have made the situation even more difficult for his daughter. The thought made him feel even worse.

'Don't.'

Matt jumped when Rachel suddenly spoke. Rolling onto his side, he felt the maelstrom of emotions inside him shift once more when he saw the sadness on her face. Obviously, she had guessed that he had doubts about what they had done and it grieved him to know that he was hurting her this way.

'I'm sorry.' He ran the tip of his finger down her cheek in gentle apology, feeling the tremor that started in the pit of his stomach when he discovered all over again how wonderfully soft her skin felt. He may have caressed every inch of her beautiful body just hours before, but touching her now, it felt like the very first time. His breath caught as he was forced to acknowledge the truth: he may have doubts about what they had done but he still wanted her. That hadn't changed.

'We didn't do anything wrong, Matt,' she said quietly, her eyes holding his. 'We're both free agents, so don't beat yourself up about last night. It's over and done with, and now we can forget all about it.'

Was that what she wanted? he wondered in gut-wrenching dismay. To forget what they had shared and how magical it had been? He searched her face but could find nothing there to make him think that she hadn't meant it. Rachel wanted to put the episode behind her and whilst he doubted if he could do that, if it was what she wanted then at the very least he had to try.

'If that's what you want, it's fine by me,' he said flatly, loath to admit how much it hurt him to comply. Last night had been a turning point in his life even though he wasn't sure if it had been a turn for the better. However, evidently it hadn't been the same for her.

Pain lanced through him and he tossed back the quilt, afraid that his feelings would become only too apparent if he remained there. 'I'd better go and have a shower. Breakfast in ten minutes. OK?'

'Fine.'

She gave him a quick smile but Matt didn't linger. There was no reason to when she had made it clear that last night had been a one-off and there wasn't going to be a repeat. The thought accompanied him back to his room, stayed with him while he showered, like a black cloud hovering over his head. He knew it was going to take time before he shrugged off the feeling of rejection and cursed his own stupidity.

He wasn't a teenager, for heaven's sake! He was a grown man and he'd had relationships before he had married. Granted, he'd not had any since Claire had died, but it had been his choice to remain celibate, just as it had been his choice to sleep with Rachel. Now he had to do as she had requested and put it behind him. It shouldn't be that difficult. One night of passion wasn't going to completely alter the course of his life. Maybe it had seemed like a milestone because it had been the first time he had slept with anyone in years, but it wouldn't be the last time. Now he had taken that first step, it would be easier the next time.

He went into the kitchen and plugged in the kettle, closing his mind to the thought that he couldn't imagine wanting any woman the way he had wanted Rachel. That was nonsense, complete and utter nonsense. It wasn't as though he was in love with Rachel, was it?

CHAPTER NINE

A WEEK passed, the longest week of Rachel's life. Although Matt was unfailingly polite whenever they spoke, he never made any reference to what had happened that night. Whilst she didn't regret sleeping with him, she did regret the fact that it had caused him so much heartache. The memory of how distraught he had looked the following morning would haunt her for a long time to come.

In an effort to minimise the stress it had caused for both of them, she avoided being alone with him as much as possible. Fortunately, her knee had healed and apart from the odd twinge, it didn't cause her any major problems. She applied herself to her job with a diligence that allowed little time for anything else. At least while she was working it stopped her thinking about Matt.

There was a team meeting scheduled for the Monday afternoon. They tried to hold a meeting most weeks, although sometimes pressure of work made it impossible. However, Matt was adamant that he wanted the meeting to go ahead that day so as soon as she had finished her lunch, Rachel made her way to the staffroom. Ross was already there, sitting beside Gemma Craven, one of their practice nurses. Pam Whiteside, the other nurse, arrived a few seconds later accompanied by two members of the reception staff, Carol Walters and Beverley Humphreys.

'I've left Dianne manning the phone,' Carol explained, hurrying over to her. 'It's been bedlam this morning and if someone doesn't stay behind to answer it, we'll be running backwards and forwards. I'll fill her in later if that's all right?'

'Fine by me,' Rachel agreed, glancing round when Fraser Kennedy, their locum, came to join them.

'I can't stay long as I'm on call this afternoon. I thought I'd take Hannah with me if you don't need her,' he added, referring to their new trainee GP, Hannah Jeffries. 'She's not been out to any house calls yet and it will be good experience for her.'

'Good idea,' someone said behind them, and Rachel felt her heart lurch when she recognised Matt's deep voice.

She hurriedly took her seat, doing her best to calm down. The others would soon realise there was something wrong if she didn't get a grip of herself. The thought of everyone in the surgery finding out what had happened steadied her and by the time Matt opened the meeting, she felt more in control.

'I know everyone's got a busy afternoon ahead so I won't waste time,' he said, glancing around. His gaze skimmed over Rachel before it moved on and she wasn't sure if she felt vexed or pleased by his indifference. While she had been torturing herself with guilt, it appeared that Matt had put the episode behind him.

'We've discovered that the locum who worked here before Fraser didn't order various tests to be carried out,' Matt informed them bluntly. 'It means that a number of patients will need to be recalled.'

A shocked murmur ran around the room as the staff exchanged horrified looks. This kind of situation was unprecedented.

'You're not serious!' Rachel exclaimed, voicing everyone's dismay.

'I'm afraid I am.'

This time his gaze landed squarely on her and remained there. Rachel felt heat course through her veins when she saw the glimmer of some emotion in his eyes. Maybe Matt wasn't as indifferent to her as he was pretending? The thought caused such turmoil inside her that she had to force herself to concentrate as he continued.

'Ross and Gemma went through the files over the weekend and pulled out any that will need to be followed up. I had a look at them this morning and from what I've seen, it's imperative that we get people back in here as soon as we can.'

'What kind of tests are we talking about?' Rachel demanded, knowing that she couldn't afford to let herself be sidetracked. It had been difficult enough to carry on knowing that Matt regretted what they had done, but it would be impossible if she allowed herself to think that he had changed his mind.

'A whole range of things,' Ross answered. 'There's one patient who was diagnosed with fibroadenosis but she wasn't sent for a mammogram to rule out the possibility of it being breast cancer. Then there's another who has angina but no blood tests were ordered. We have no idea if his angina is linked to anaemia or possibly an over-production of thyroid hormones.'

'But that's unforgivable!' Fraser exploded. 'Those tests are purely routine, so why on earth didn't the fellow make sure they were done?'

'Probably because he couldn't be bothered completing the paperwork.' Matt's tone was harsh. 'I'm sure those of us who worked with him remember how he was always bragging that he could get through his lists faster than anyone else could do. Little wonder when he was doing only half the job.'

Dianne poked her head round the door just then to tell Ross there was a phone call for him in Reception and he excused himself.

Fraser announced that he and Hannah would have to leave too and followed him out. Matt explained to the others that he would let everyone know how he intended to handle the recalls and the meeting broke up, but Rachel didn't leave with the others. She could tell how worried Matt was about this development and couldn't bear to leave him to deal with the problem by himself.

'How many people will we need to recall, do you know?' she asked.

'At the moment it stands at just over three dozen, although I'll go through the case notes again in case anyone's been missed out.'

'Do you really need to do that?' she protested. 'If Ross and Gemma have checked the files then I can't see that they'll have overlooked anyone.'

'Probably not, but at the end of the day I'm responsible for the patients who are registered with this practice so it's down to me to make sure that everyone who needs to be recalled is seen.'

Rachel sighed. 'I've said this before, Matt, but you can't be responsible for every single thing that happens here. It's too much for anyone, including you.'

'That may be so, but it doesn't alter the fact that ultimately I'm to blame if things go wrong.' He shrugged. 'Anyway, I prefer to do the job myself. That way I'm not disappointed if other people don't come up to my expectations.'

'I used to think like that, too, was always afraid of being let down. But sometimes you have to take a risk and trust people.' Rachel could hear the plea in her voice. They may have been discussing the running of the surgery but she was aware that their comments could apply to more than their work. If Matt would take a risk in his private life, she thought sadly, his life could be very different.

The realisation that she would probably never be a part of his life even if he did so was too hard to bear. Rachel excused herself and left, feeling a sense of loss welling up inside her. That night they had spent together had made her long for more, more nights and days too. The truth was that she wanted Matt in her life week in and week out, year after year, and the thought brought a rush of tears to her eyes because it was unlikely to happen. Matt may have enjoyed making love to her but he didn't want her to play a permanent role in his future. He couldn't do when he so obviously regretted what had gone on.

Rachel went back to her room, forcing down the tide of emotions that threatened to engulf her. She wouldn't cry, not now, not here. Here in the surgery she had a role to fulfil and she would do it to the best of her ability. She wasn't a woman with a bruised and battered heart but a doctor who had patients who relied on her.

It was something to cling to, what gave her life purpose even though it was no longer enough to fill it the way it had done in the past. Now that she knew how good it felt to love someone, she longed for more, but if it wasn't to be, she had to accept that. She certainly couldn't make Matt love her in return and wouldn't try. For love to mean anything it had to be true to itself—it couldn't be forced or coerced.

Matt understood that because he had loved his late wife. Maybe one day he would reach a point where he could move on, but it wouldn't be her, Rachel Mackenzie, he gave his heart to. It would be some other woman who reaped that reward.

Matt could feel that black cloud hovering over him again all afternoon long. It was partly the fact that it felt as though everything was falling apart around him, but mainly because Rachel had been so distant towards him recently. Even that afternoon, when he would have expected her to help him thrash out this problem, she had made an excuse and left. She was determined to put their night of passion behind her and he wished he could do the same. Oh, he had tried all right, but he knew to his cost how spectacularly unsuccessful he had been. He merely had to be near her and his body was instantly on the alert, as it had been that day!

Matt cursed under his breath as he checked that all the lights were off and locked up. He got into his car and headed for home, taking his time as the roads were extremely busy. With less than a week to go before Christmas, the shops were staying open late and that explained all the extra traffic. He reached the centre of town at last and joined the queue at the intersection to wait for the lights to change, inching his way forward until there was just one car in front of him.

The lights changed again and the car ahead of him moved forward. It was halfway across the junction when a van came hurtling out of one of the side roads, ignoring the fact that the traffic lights were against it. It rammed into the car and sent it spinning across the road where it came to rest wedged up against a lamppost. The van didn't stop but sped on, clipping the sides of several other vehicles that were waiting to enter the multi-storey car park as it hurtled off down the road.

Unsurprisingly, there was chaos after that. People were leaping out of their cars to see what damage had been done, bringing the traffic to a standstill. Matt ignored what was going on around him as he leapt out of his car and ran across the road to where the first car had ended up. There were two girls in it and he could tell at once that both were injured. A middle-aged man suddenly pushed past him and wrenched open the passenger side door, obviously intending to lift the nearest girl out, and Matt hurriedly intervened.

'Don't move her!' he ordered, elbowing the man aside. Crouching down, he checked the girl's pulse and was relieved when he found it to be rather rapid but reassuringly strong. She had a nasty cut on the side of her head just above her left ear which he guessed had happened when the side window had shattered. She was obviously shocked and disorientated, but apart from that she didn't appear to be too badly injured. However, one thing he had learned over the years was never to take anything at face value. He turned to the other man.

'I'm a doctor and although I don't think she's too badly injured, I don't want her moved until I'm sure it's safe to do so. Can you stand here while I check the driver and stop anyone else from moving her?'

The man looked doubtful. He was obviously loath to follow Matt's instructions until a woman in the crowd suddenly piped up. 'You do what Dr Thompson tells you, Alf. He's the expert so don't you go moving her until he says so.'

Matt silently blessed her as he hurried round the car to check on the driver, a girl in her teens who looked scarcely old enough to hold a licence. The driver's door was crumpled in and it was impossible to open it, but with the help of a bystander, he managed to force open the hatchback and climbed into the car that way. There wasn't much room to manoeuvre as the driver's seat had broken in two and the top half was resting on the rear seat.

Matt inched himself forward as far as he could go and placed his fingers on the carotid artery in the girl's neck. His heart sank because he couldn't detect a pulse at first. He tried again and finally felt the tiniest flutter beneath his fingertips. She was alive but only just from the look of it.

'Matt?'

He looked round when he heard a familiar voice calling him and felt his heart lift when he saw Rachel peering through the open hatch-back. 'Good timing! I could do with some help,' he said, trying not to let her know how pleased he was to see her. Rachel had made no bones about the fact that she wasn't looking for commitment and that night they had spent to-gether had proved it beyond any doubt. She couldn't have dismissed what had happened so easily if it had meant anything to her.

He forced the thought to the back of his mind because it was neither the time nor the place to dwell on it. Leaning forward, he tried to assess the girl's injuries, but it was impos-sible to see very much. It appeared that her legs had been trapped when the car's bonnet had been crushed and he simply couldn't tell how serious her injuries were.

'Damn!' he cursed, carefully easing his way back out of the vehicle. It was an old car and it hadn't stood much of a chance when the van had hit it. There were chunks of metal protruding into the interior and they proved a major hazard when getting in and out. He finally made it unscathed and turned to Rachel, trying not to notice how pretty she looked in the glow from the streetlamps.

'She's alive but that's about all I can tell you. I can't assess how badly injured she is because I can't get to her. However, her pulse is very faint. If I had to hazard a guess, I'd say she's bleeding internally.'

'Maybe I can get a better look,' Rachel suggested. 'I'm smaller than you and I should be able to wriggle further into the car.'

'It's worth a try,' he agreed. 'But be careful.

There's chunks of metal sticking out all over the place—you don't want to cut yourself.'

'I certainly don't.' Rachel shrugged off her coat and handed it to him. 'It will be easier without this and we can use it to cover her up with once I've examined her. It's freezing tonight and she needs to be kept warm.'

She climbed into the car and Matt found himself holding his breath as he watched her lean through the gap between the front seats. Part of the front axle had broken through the floor and there were a lot of sharp pieces of metal about.

'Careful!' he warned. 'Mind where you put your hands.'

Rachel nodded, preferring to save her breath for the difficult task of inching herself far enough forward to reach the lower half of the girl's body. Matt caught a tantalising glimpse of her shapely bottom before he averted his eyes. He made his way round to the passenger side to check on the other casualty. She seemed a little less shocked, he noted in relief, although he put out a restraining hand when she tried to unbuckle her seat belt.

'Just give me a moment to check you over before you try to move. We don't want you doing yourself any more damage, do we?'

'It was that van driver's fault, not Katie's,' the girl said shakily. 'He came racing through the lights on red…' She gulped as she cast a look at her friend, although with Rachel in the middle of the seats she couldn't see her clearly.

'I know. I was in the car behind you and I saw what happened,' Matt said soothingly, checking her pulse again. 'I'm a doctor, by the way. My name's Matthew Thompson and the lady in the middle is also a doctor. Her name is Rachel Mackenzie. We both work at Dalverston Surgery.'

'Oh, you're my mum's doctor! She's always

singing your praises and saying how lovely you are!' the girl exclaimed, then blushed.

'Thank you kindly. It's always good to know that you don't scare your patients.' Matt smiled at her. 'So what's your name? I don't remember seeing you in the surgery.'

'Megan Bradley, and you haven't seen me 'cos I haven't been ill since we moved here.' She grimaced. 'Not up till now, anyway.'

'Well, if it's any consolation, Megan, I don't think you're badly injured from what I can tell,' he assured her. 'But you're the best person to know how you feel. Is there anywhere that hurts really badly?'

'Just my ribs. They sort of ache but I expect it's because of the seat belt.' Tears welled up in her eyes all of a sudden. 'Katie's been hurt far more than me, hasn't she?'

'I'm afraid so.' Matt ran a gentle hand down the girl's spine to check for any signs of misalignment in the vertebrae. From what he could tell, everything was fine and he nodded. 'Right, we're going to get you out of there but we're going to do it really slowly, understand?'

'Like they do in those TV series?' Megan asked him.

'Exactly like that,' he agreed, inwardly blessing the writers of the popular dramas. The general public's knowledge had increased tenfold thanks to a steady diet of medical soap operas and in his view that was a good thing.

'I've a collar in my bag and I'm going to put it around your neck to protect the top of your spine. It will feel a little uncomfortable but it's worth wearing it.'

'I don't mind,' Megan assured him. 'I'm hoping to train as a nurse when I leave school next year so it will be good practice for me to know how it feels.'

'Definitely!' Matt gave her a warm smile,

thanking his lucky stars that she was obviously a practical girl and not given to hysterics. It made his job that much easier.

He stood up and hurried over to his car. He hadn't got round to unpacking all the extra equipment he had taken with him to that incident at the canal, which was fortunate. He sighed as he found a collar plus everything he needed to set up a drip for the young driver. It felt like years had passed since that day. So much had happened since then that it felt as though he had packed in several years worth of living.

His gaze moved to Rachel as he headed back across the road and he felt an ache of such intensity start up inside him that he had to pause. He could lie to himself but what was the point? Since Claire had died he had been merely going through the motions of living. That night he and Rachel had spent together had proved that to him. It wasn't what Claire would have wanted, either. She would have been appalled, in fact. Claire would have hated to think of him wasting his life the way he had been doing. She would have wanted him to be happy.

Matt started walking again and it felt as though he was leaving the past behind him at last. He had no regrets, strangely enough, because that had been then and this was now, although what the future held was another matter. Nobody could foretell what lay in store for them and he was glad. He didn't want to look too far ahead in case he was disappointed. He just wanted to enjoy what he had now.

His gaze rested on Rachel as he drew closer and he felt warmth well up inside him because at this very moment he had Rachel here beside him.

CHAPTER TEN

IT WAS well over an hour before the emergency services finally managed to free the injured driver. It had been a very difficult and complicated task as the firemen had needed to remove the engine as well as the roof of the car. Matt had insisted on remaining in the car while the work had been carried out, monitoring the girl's condition and reassuring her as she had drifted in and out of consciousness.

Once Katie had been lifted out of the vehicle, the paramedics hurriedly transferred her to an ambulance. Rachel sighed as she watched it drive away with its siren blaring and its lights flashing. The girl had a fractured pelvis, which explained the massive blood loss she'd suffered, and there was bound to be internal injuries too. Although everyone had done all they possibly could, it was touch and go whether she would pull through.

'I think it's a case of crossing our fingers and hoping, don't you?'

Matt came back from giving a statement to the police. Rachel nodded when she heard what he said. It had been more or less what she had been thinking too. 'How do you rate her chances?'

'Not all that high, I'm afraid.' He shrugged, his handsome face looking very grim. 'If the fire brigade had been able to get her out sooner, she would have stood a much better chance.'

'They did their best,' Rachel replied, watching a couple of the crew from the local fire station gathering together the equipment they had used.

'They did, and it wasn't meant as a criticism. Nobody could have got her out of that car any faster. It was in such a bad state. However, it doesn't alter the fact that the delay is bound to have affected her chances of survival.'

His voice sounded flat but Rachel understood why. To see a young life possibly cut short this way was always distressing. Without pausing to think, she laid her hand on his arm. 'She still has a chance, Matt. The fact that you were here when the accident happened and were able to give her immediate assistance is bound to have worked in her favour.'

'Thank you. That makes me feel a lot better, although I can't take all the credit. You did more than your share, Rachel. I would never have been able to set up that drip without your help.' He smiled at her, his eyes filling with a warmth that immediately made her feel warm too. 'It was a real team effort.'

'I suppose so.' Rachel hurriedly removed her hand. She couldn't afford to start hoping that his smile might mean anything. She grimaced as she looked around at the scene of chaos that surrounded them. There were vehicles scattered all over the place and people standing in the road. Nobody was being allowed to leave until they had been questioned by the police whose main priority now was to find the van driver who had caused the accident. 'What a mess!'

'It'll take a while to sort it all out by the look of it,' Matt observed.

'It will.' Rachel sighed as she turned and looked at the multi-storey car park. 'Heaven only knows when I'll be able to get my car out of the car park. The exit is completely blocked by traffic and there's a huge tailback of cars along all the ramps. It's going to take ages to clear them away.'

'It is.' Matt frowned as he studied the

build-up of traffic. 'Have you finished all your shopping?'

'More or less. To be honest, I don't really feel like doing any more tonight,' she admitted.

'Then why don't you leave your car where it is and let me drive you home?' He pointed across the road to where his car was still standing in the same spot he had abandoned it well over an hour before. 'I've given the police a statement and I'm free to leave. It seems pointless for you to hang around here when I can give you a lift, doesn't it?'

It did and Rachel was tempted, very tempted indeed. However, would it be wise to accept the offer after what had happened since that night they had slept together? She had done her best to stay out of Matt's way and allowing him to drive her home certainly wasn't the best way to maintain her distance.

'It's kind of you, Matt, but I'm not sure if it's safe to leave my car there overnight.'

He sighed heavily. 'I doubt if that's the real reason, is it? Look, Rachel, I know you're keen to forget what happened between us that night—you've made that perfectly plain. However, all I'm offering you is a lift home, nothing more.'

Rachel flushed, embarrassed by his bluntness. 'It just seemed better to give you some space,' she said quietly. 'I could tell you were upset about what we'd done the following morning and I didn't want to make the situation even more difficult for you.'

'I appreciate that, although I think you were just as keen to put it behind you,' he said flatly, and she frowned when she heard the echo of hurt in his voice.

'In a way, yes, I was, but not because I regretted what we'd done. I just don't want you getting hurt, Matt. That's all.'

'And here I was thinking that you didn't give a damn. How wrong could I be?' He

smiled at her, his eyes filled with such tenderness that some of the ice that had filled her
heart started to melt. Was it possible that they
had been at cross-purposes?

The thought was way too enticing. Rachel
bit her lip, afraid of what she might say if she
allowed herself to speak. Matt brushed her
cheek with his knuckles and she could feel
the tremor that passed through him as his
fingers glided over her skin.

'I think we need to talk, Rachel, don't you?
Let me drive you home and see if we can
sort this out.'

Rachel nodded, surprised to find that now
she couldn't have forced out a single word.
She followed him across the road to his car
and settled herself in the passenger seat and
still she didn't say anything. She had no idea
how they were going to resolve this problem
if she was still struck dumb when they
reached his house, but it didn't seem to

matter. The fact that Matt cared enough to want to clear up this misunderstanding far outweighed everything else.

It took them a bare ten minutes to reach Matt's house. He drew up outside the front door and turned to look at her. 'Are you all right here? We can go to yours if you'd feel more comfortable there. I should have checked with you before.'

'No, here is fine,' she replied, trying to control the tide of heat that threatened to engulf her. Was he remembering what had happened the last time she had been in his home? Recalling in exquisite, exhilarating detail their love-making and how wonderful it had been?

Her legs felt as though they had turned to jelly as she followed him into the house. It wasn't surprising either when her mind was busily unreeling a whole series of tantalising images, pictures of them lying together, their limbs entwined, their bodies fused in the most intimate fashion possible. Matt had been the most ardent and yet the gentlest of lovers and she knew that she would never experience the joy he had shown her that night with anyone else. She couldn't do. It was only Matt she wanted, only him she loved.

The realisation filled her with joy but it also scared her. It made her see just how very vulnerable she was.

Matt could hear his heart thumping as he led the way into the kitchen and switched on the lights. It was making such a racket that he would be amazed if Rachel couldn't hear it too. He glanced at her as he plugged in the kettle but her face gave away very little about her feelings. In fact, she looked ever so slightly stunned, as though she had suffered a shock and was desperately trying to deal with it.

He grimaced as he reached for the jar of

coffee. They had just attended a major accident so was it any wonder if she felt shocked? What she needed at this moment was a cup of coffee and some time to get herself together before they talked about them.

His heart gave another noisy drum roll at the word 'them' and he gritted his teeth. There wasn't a *them*, at least not yet there wasn't. There was Rachel and there was him, and just because they'd had sex it didn't make them a couple, not even when it had been the most mind-blowing sex he had ever experienced!

Heat scorched through his veins and he hurriedly applied himself to making the coffee as he fought to get a grip on himself. Making love with Rachel had been a truly memorable experience, but he was only flesh and blood and he had needs like any other man, needs that he had suppressed for a very long time. It was hardly surprising their love-making had been such a huge success, bearing all that in mind.

It was the most logical explanation, even though in his heart Matt had great difficulty believing it was the real reason why making love with Rachel had been so wonderful. However, he couldn't afford to let himself get carried away when they needed to talk everything through.

He poured the coffee, placing the mugs on the kitchen table because it would seem less intimate if they talked in here rather than in the sitting room. Soft lights and a crackling fire were all well and good, he thought as he went to fetch the milk out of the fridge, but he hadn't brought Rachel here to seduce her…Well, not consciously, although the idea was *very* tempting now that he thought about it.

His mind drifted off before he could stop it, soaking up the delights of firelight flickering on smooth alabaster skin, and he groaned under his breath. Now, that really was too much temptation for any man!

'Matt?'

Rachel's voice roused him and he realised that he had missed what she had said. 'Sorry. I was miles away,' he apologised as he placed the milk jug on the table and sat down. 'What did you say?'

'Worrying about that poor girl, I expect.' She sighed, completely misinterpreting the reason for his abstraction. 'I do hope she's all right.'

'So do I, although I wasn't actually thinking about her. I was thinking about us.' He added some milk to his coffee, wondering if he was mad to admit it, but he refused to lie. There had been enough misunderstandings recently without deliberately creating any more.

'Oh! I see,' she said shakily and he felt his heart swell with tenderness when he heard the breathless note in her voice. It was obvious that it was as important to Rachel as it was to him to sort out this mess.

The thought gave a welcome boost to his

courage and he carried on. 'I know that night we spent together has changed things, Rachel. And you were right to say that I was upset the following morning because it's true. However, it doesn't mean that I regret sleeping with you.'

He paused, needing a moment to work out the best way to explain how he had felt. He wasn't used to opening his heart this way but he knew that he owed her the truth and nothing less. 'Making love with you was wonderful, *you* were wonderful. If I was upset afterwards it was because I couldn't help feeling that I had let Claire down in some way.'

'It must be hard for you, Matt. I know what a wonderful marriage you had. I can't imagine how difficult it must have been for you when you lost Claire. I…I've never loved anyone that much.'

There was something in her voice that brought his eyes to her face but she wasn't looking at him. She was staring down at her cup, making it impossible for him to see her expression clearly. Matt frowned. Had there been a hint of doubt in that claim she had made about never having really loved anyone? he wondered, then immediately dismissed the idea. There was no reason for her to lie to him, was there?

'It was difficult. The only way I could cope was by focussing on my job and taking care of Heather. However, Heather is all grown up now and she no longer needs me to look after her.' He smiled ruefully. 'I don't think she's needed me to do so for some time, but she knew I needed her. That's why she came back to Dalverston after she finished her nurse's training.'

'Heather loves you, Matt. She wouldn't have seen it as a hardship to come back here.'

'How did you know what I was thinking?' he exclaimed.

'Because I've often wondered the same thing myself about Ross. Did he decide to settle in Dalverston because of me?' She laughed softly. 'He would never admit it, of course!'

'Maybe not but his actions speak for themselves, don't they? Ross chose to live here because he loves you, Rachel, and he appreciates how hard you've worked to bring him up.' He reached across the table and squeezed her hand. 'You've been a wonderful mother to him.'

'Thank you for saying that. It means such a lot to me.'

Tears glistened in her eyes before she blinked them away. Matt released her hand and picked up his cup, giving her a moment to collect herself. They were here to talk about their relationship, not their respective roles as parents.

Once again his heart clamoured at the thought of them having a relationship and this time he didn't correct himself. He and Rachel did have a relationship. They'd had one for a number of years and it had been a highly successful one too. The fact that it had altered recently was the sticking point and they needed to decide what they were going to do about it.

Matt drank his coffee, wondering how to raise the subject in a way that wouldn't cause Rachel any embarrassment. Coming straight out and asking her how she felt about them having an affair seemed so crass but that was what it amounted to. He wasn't ready yet to offer her anything more, although at some point in the future…

He cut short that thought before it could run away with him. 'Look, Rachel,' he began.

'How do you feel about us trying again?'

They both spoke at once and both stopped. Matt took a deep breath as he felt his head reel. That Rachel should have suggested what he'd been going to say stunned him. He was still trying to work out how to reply when she continued.

'If what happened was a one-off, Matt, then fine. I understand. But if you feel that one night wasn't enough, I think you need to be totally upfront about that too.'

'How do you feel about it?' he said, his voice sounding hoarse.

She shrugged. 'I asked first.'

Oh, hell! This was difficult, more difficult than anything he had ever done before. Matt's blood pressure rose until it felt as though he was going to burst from the pressure building up inside him. And yet in his heart he knew there was only one answer, only one *truthful* answer, at least. He refused to be a coward and lie to her about something as important as this.

'One night wasn't enough for me, Rachel. It never could be enough when I felt things that night that I've never felt before.'

His eyes held hers fast and he saw her pupils dilate when she realised what he was saying, that not even with Claire had he felt the way he had felt when he had made love to her. For a moment all the old guilt came rushing back and swamped him and then, miraculously, his head cleared. All he could think about was Rachel and what she was offering him, something so precious that he would be a fool to turn it down.

Capturing her hands, he pulled her to her feet and drew her into his arms, holding her so close that he could feel the firm swell of her breasts pushing against his chest, feel the exact moment when her nipples hardened with desire. His own body quickened and he heard her suck in a sharp little breath when she realised he was aroused too and didn't give a damn. He was past pretending, way past the point of playing games.

'I don't know how long this will last,

Rachel, and I don't care. I just know that I want you more than I've wanted anyone in a very long time.'

'I'm not asking you for a guarantee, Matt,' she whispered. 'Nobody can foretell how long a relationship will last.'

'No, they can't,' he agreed, refusing to think about how devastated he would be if he lost her. 'But what I can do is promise you on my honour that whatever happens we will deal with it like two sensible adults.'

'Can you really be sensible when you feel like this?' she murmured, moving her hips against his and making him groan.

'No, I can't. I don't even want to try. I just want to make mad, passionate love to you right here and right now. Is it enough to be going on with?'

'Yes. More than enough for me.'

Reaching up on tiptoe, she pressed her mouth to his, her lips parting to invite his to open too. Matt felt the rush of desire hit him like a sledgehammer as he pulled her hard against him, letting her feel in intimate detail exactly what she was doing to him. The coffee cups went flying as he lifted her onto the table but he didn't care. What did some broken china matter when his heart was being healed?

They made love right there in the kitchen and it was even better than the first time, amazingly enough. Matt knew that he scaled new heights that night and that he couldn't have done that with anyone but Rachel. As her body opened to him, he realised that he was on the brink of falling in love with her, but he also knew it was a step too far at this stage. Rachel hadn't asked for love or commitment, just that they be together. He had to be content with that. For now.

They climaxed together, crying out each other's name in unison, and even if it wasn't an omen for the future, it proved they had made the right decision at this moment. He could live with that, live in the present and enjoy what he had. He only hoped Rachel could do so too for a very long time.

Matt was still asleep when Rachel got up the following morning. It was very early and the central heating hadn't switched itself on yet. She shivered as she unhooked his robe from the behind the bedroom door and pulled it on. It was far too big for her but she rolled up the sleeves and tightened the belt around her waist. The real bonus apart from an immediate feeling of warmth was that it smelled of Matt and she sniffed appreciatively as she made her way down the stairs. Being enveloped in his scent might not be as good as being held in his arms but it was the next best thing.

A smile curled her mouth as she set to work

to make them some breakfast. The bacon was crisping and the eggs were sizzling by the time Matt appeared looking wonderfully sexy as he padded into the kitchen wearing nothing more than a pair of boxer shorts. He grinned as he came over to her and pulled her into his arms.

'Aha, so you're the culprit.'

'I am?' Rachel smiled into his eyes, loving the way his hair fell in a disorderly wave onto his forehead. Matt was normally impeccably groomed and it was a rare and pleasant surprise to see him looking less than perfect for once.

She brushed the lock of hair back into its rightful place, revelling in the fact that she had the right to enjoy such intimacies. 'You'll have to enlighten me. What is it I'm supposed to have done?'

'Oh, there's no supposed about it, not when the evidence is clear to see.' His hands went to the belt on the robe. 'You, Dr Mackenzie, stole my dressing gown and for that you deserve to be suitably punished.'

'Oh, but I didn't *steal* it,' Rachel objected, keen to point out that she had merely borrowed it. However, it appeared that Matt wasn't interested in hearing her defence.

He peeled the robe off her and tossed it aside, his mouth claiming hers in a drugging kiss that made her forget every argument she had been about to make. When he pressed her back against the wall, she didn't protest but gave in willingly. It felt so good to have him kiss her, hold her and make her his. Their love-making would have reached its natural conclusion if the sudden shrilling of an angry smoke alarm hadn't interrupted them.

Matt chuckled as he let her go and switched off the gas. 'Looks as though the bacon has gone for a burton.'

'And the eggs.' Rachel shook her head as she poked at the blackened remains in the frying pan. 'You do realise that you've missed out on having breakfast in bed?'

'That's a shame, although I have to confess that I prefer the alternative.'

He leered comically at her and she laughed as she aimed a playful cuff at his ear. 'You are completely shameless, Matthew Thompson!'

'Good. It's music to my ears to hear you say that. I was in danger of turning into a real old fuddy-duddy and I rather like the idea of being seen as someone whose attitude to life is a bit more risqué.'

'Fuddy-duddy! No way could you be described as that. According to my friends, you're a real babe.'

'Is that a fact?' He grinned at her. 'Whilst I feel I should point out that I'm a tad long in the tooth to be called a babe, I certainly won't dispute it. However, what interests me most of all is if you agree with your friends. Do you?'

'Now, *that* would be telling!'

Rachel shot past him as she beat a hasty retreat. Matt was hard on her heels as she flew up the stairs but, then, she wasn't trying all that hard to outrun him. They made love in his bedroom then took a shower together and made love in there too and it was wonderful again. Rachel had never enjoyed this kind of closeness with anyone before and revelled in it. She could get used to living like this, she thought later as she got dressed, very used to waking up with Matt each morning and falling asleep beside him each night. However, she had to remember that this wasn't for ever but just for now.

She sighed as she finished buttoning up her blouse. She may have found her soulmate, but it took two people to build a lasting relationship. She had absolutely no experience of making a lifelong commitment, although she could learn. As for Matt, he had the experience because he had done it before, but she didn't know yet if he would want to do it all over again with her. All she could do was hope that he would.

CHAPTER ELEVEN

MATT was amazed by how happy he felt in the days that followed. Not even the problems they were currently experiencing at the surgery seemed to trouble him the way they once would have done. He knew it was all down to his relationship with Rachel.

It had added a new dimension to his life, one that had been missing for far too long, and he found himself praying that it would continue. Maybe they hadn't made a commitment but what they did have felt so right that he never wanted it to end. The idea that he was falling in love with her crossed his mind with increasing frequency but he didn't allow himself to dwell on it. He was afraid that he would spoil things if he wished for more than he had. Although Rachel hadn't moved in with him, she spent most nights at his house and their sex life continued to be amazing. He kept wondering if a time would arrive when they settled into a routine but it never happened. Each time they made love it felt as though it was the first time and it blew his mind.

Christmas came, the best Christmas he could remember in years. Ross joined them for lunch and although he didn't say anything, Matt had a feeling that Ross had guessed there was something going on between him and Rachel. He also got the impression that Ross was genuinely pleased for them and it was a relief to know that their relationship wasn't going to create problems in that area. When Heather phoned to wish him a happy Christmas, he was tempted to tell her about

Rachel but something held him back. Maybe it would be safer not to tempt fate.

After Christmas it was time to finish sorting out the mess created by their former locum. They had managed to whittle down the number of recalls to just half a dozen by then. Alison Bradshaw, the woman who had been diagnosed with fibroadenosis, was his first appointment when he returned to work after the festive break. She'd been on holiday when they had tried to contact her and that had caused an added delay. Matt brought up her file on the computer and was reading through the decidedly scrappy notes the locum had made when Rachel tapped on his door.

'You look very industrious. Heavy list this morning?'

'About average for this time of the year.' Matt tipped back his chair and smiled at her, wondering if he would ever reach a point where he felt indifferent to her. It was just over an hour since they had got out of bed yet his heart was already kicking up a storm.

Rachel closed the door and came around the desk to drop a kiss on his lips. They had agreed to keep their relationship a secret from their colleagues. Neither of them relished the thought of being gossiped about so they were very discreet when they were at work. That Rachel had broken their rules and kissed him made his heart race with delight.

'I thought you might need a top-up to help you through the morning.'

'Mmm, I do. I do.' Matt pulled her down onto his lap and kissed her soundly, smiling when she eagerly responded. He loved the fact that she never pretended but let him know exactly how she felt. He scattered a shower of butterfly-soft kisses over her face and neck then reluctantly drew back. 'That will have to keep me going until lunchtime, although I'll probably need another top-up by then.'

'Always happy to help out a colleague in need,' she replied saucily, laughing at him.

That remark would have prompted a reprisal if the buzzer on his desk hadn't sounded to warn him his first appointment was waiting in Reception. Matt groaned as he tipped her off his knee. 'Action stations. It's time to knuckle down to some work.'

'Aye, aye, Captain!'

Rachel saluted smartly then headed for the door, leaving him chuckling. She had that effect on him, made him feel more positive about life than he had felt in ages. She was everything he admired in a woman—warm, caring, sexy…

He made himself stop right there, knowing from experience how fast his thoughts could run away with him. He called in Alison Bradshaw and set about explaining why he wanted to send her for a mammogram. She was naturally worried so he phoned up the hospital and made an appointment for her to be seen the following week.

Thankfully, her symptoms had settled down and on checking her breasts, he found nothing to indicate there might be a problem. However, he would only truly relax when the results of the mammogram came back and proved that everything was clear.

He saw her out and worked his way through the rest of his list. His last patient had just left when Carol phoned with a query about someone else who was on the recall list. Matt told her that he would come to the office to sort it out and gathered up the case notes he'd used. He was just walking along the corridor when a girl came out of the treatment room and he paused when he realised it was Megan Bradley, the passenger in the car that had been involved in that accident in the town centre.

'Hello! What are you doing here?'

'Having my stitches out,' Megan explained,

pushing back her hair so that he could see the thin red scar above her ear. 'I was dreading having it done in case it hurt, but the nurse was so gentle I hardly felt a thing.'

'Good.' Matt smiled at her. 'So you're fully recovered, are you?'

'Yes, thank you. I felt a bit shaky for a few days afterwards and my head hurt but all things considered I got off very lightly.'

'And what about your friend who was driving—Katie? I telephoned the hospital and know that she came through the operation to repair her pelvis. Is she making good progress?'

'Not too bad, but it will be a while before she's up and about again.' Mel sighed. 'The police still haven't found the van driver. They were able to trace who owned the van from the CCTV pictures but it had been reported as stolen a couple of days before the accident. I hate to think the driver is going to get away with it after all the damage he's caused.'

'I'm sure the police will track him down eventually,' Matt said soothingly. 'The main thing is that both you and Katie are going to be all right.'

'You're right, Dr Mackenzie. Of course you are.'

Mel gave him a beaming smile and left. Matt went to the office and sorted out Carol's query in a buoyant mood. It was good to know that both girls would recover from their ordeal. The upside of feeling so happy himself was that he wanted only good things to happen for everyone else. He certainly didn't want any disasters to spoil what he and Rachel had now or in the future.

He frowned as he went back to his room. Once again he was thinking long term and it wasn't wise to do that. All he could do was hope that their relationship meant as much to Rachel as it meant to him.

* * *

It was the most wonderful time of Rachel's entire life. She couldn't remember when she had felt so happy before. Being with Matt both in and out of work was like a dream come true.

Amazingly their professional relationship didn't suffer. Matt still treated her with the same respect and courtesy when they were in the surgery, even if the look in his eyes did raise matters onto a very different plane! Rachel knew without the shadow of a doubt that she had found the man she wanted to spend her life with. However, until Matt admitted that he felt the same way, she mustn't get carried away.

The thought of what might happen in the future was the only blot on the horizon and she refused to let it ruin things. Thankfully she was so busy that she had very little time to dwell on it. Having to fit in the patients they needed to recall meant they were all pushed to the limit. Morning and evening lists were longer than ever.

Then there was a near crisis when their practice nurse, Gemma Craven, attended a call at one of the outlying farms and got lost in a snowstorm. Rachel was surprised when she saw how worried Ross was when Gemma went missing. It made her wonder if there was something going on between them. Quite frankly, she would be glad if there was because Ross deserved to be happy and Gemma was a lovely girl. She was tempted to ask him but in the end decided that she wouldn't interfere. She knew how it felt to want to protect a new and very precious relationship.

It was the beginning of February when Rachel discovered that something had happened that was bound to affect her relationship with Matt. She had been feeling off-colour for several days, nauseous and dizzy, and had put it down to that wretched bug that was still doing the rounds. However, when she was violently sick one morning as she got up, she was forced to consider some other options and was shocked by what she came up with. Was it possible that she was pregnant?

She hurried back to the bedroom and took her diary out of her bag. Although it was normal for a woman's menstrual cycle to alter as she approached the menopause, hers had been remarkably regular up till now. However on checking the date, she realised that her period was almost two weeks late. She tried to tell herself that there was no need to panic but she couldn't help adding everything up, the dizziness and nausea, the bout of sickness that morning and the missed period, and they all pointed towards the same conclusion: she could be pregnant.

Rachel's head was reeling as she went downstairs. She was forty-six years old and she couldn't have a baby at her age! It wasn't as though she and Matt had taken any chances either because they had always used contraception. However, as a doctor she knew only too well that no contraceptive was one hundred per cent guaranteed. Her heart sank as she sat down at the kitchen table and wondered how Matt would react if she told him of her suspicions. She couldn't imagine he would be pleased when he had made it clear that he wasn't looking for commitment. After all, a child was the ultimate commitment of all.

'Are you feeling all right, sweetheart? You look awfully pale this morning.'

Matt came and crouched down beside her, his face filled with such concern that Rachel was hard pressed not to bawl her eyes out. Becoming a father again at this stage in his life would be the last thing he'd choose.

'I think I may be coming down with that bug that's been doing the rounds,' she murmured, hating the fact that she had to lie to him, although she had no choice. She needed to find out if she really was pregnant before she said anything. She dredged up a watery smile. 'I feel really rotten, if I'm honest.'

'Then there's no way that you're going into work today,' he said firmly. He got up and poured her a cup of tea then helped her to her feet. 'It's back to bed for you. Doctor's orders!'

Rachel laughed but there was a hollow ring to it. She allowed him to help her back up the stairs and lay down obediently on the bed. He placed the cup of tea on the bedside table then bent and brushed her forehead with a gentle kiss.

'Stay there and try to sleep. I'll pop back at lunchtime to see if you're all right.' He took the phone out of its charger and placed it on the pillow beside her. 'Phone me if you feel any worse, though. Promise?'

'Promise,' Rachel whispered, wondering if it was possible to feel any worse than she did. Tears trickled from her eyes and she turned her face into the pillow so that he wouldn't see her crying as he left the room. She had never felt more desolate in her life, not even when she had found out that she was expecting Ross.

As soon as Matt had left for work she got dressed and drove into town to buy a pregnancy testing kit. She took it back to her own home and did the test there. Waiting for the results was agonising but finally she had confirmation that her suspicions were correct. She was pregnant and now she needed to decide what she was going to do.

At her age there were added risks to having a baby and she would need to undergo various tests if she went ahead with the pregnancy. Nobody would blame her if she decided not to go through with it, yet she shied away from the idea of having a termination. How she was going to tell Matt was something she still hadn't worked out. It would have been different if they had made a real commitment to each other but their relationship was founded on the here and now, and she certainly wouldn't *blackmail* him into staying with her because of their child.

Matt had a highly developed sense of duty and she knew that he would feel he had to support her if they were still together when she broke the news to him. She couldn't bear to think that he could end up resenting her one day. Tears stung her eyes but she really didn't have a choice. It would be better to end things now than run the risk of that happening.

Matt couldn't stop worrying about Rachel all morning long. Her illness seemed to have come on remarkably quickly even if it was that wretched bug. He waited until there was a gap between patients and phoned the house, feeling more concerned than ever when there was no reply. Surely she must have heard the phone ringing, he thought as he replaced the receiver. So why hadn't she answered it?

He tried telling himself that she was probably fast asleep but he could barely wait for lunchtime to arrive. There was another delay then because the results of various tests had come back and he needed to check them. The results of Alison Bradshaw's mammogram were amongst them and he was relieved to see that it was clear. He asked Carol to phone Alison to make sure she'd received a copy then made his escape before anything else could delay him.

He drove straight home, frowning when he discovered that Rachel's car had gone. Had she felt better and decided to go home? He set off down the lane, letting out a sigh of relief when he saw her car parked outside the cottage. Although he had no idea why she had come back to her own home, at least she was safe.

Rachel opened the door to his knock but

instead of inviting him in, she just stood and looked at him. Matt wasn't sure what was going on but it was obvious that there was something very wrong and his insides churned in sudden apprehension. It took every scrap of willpower he possessed to smile at her when it felt as though his world was on the brink of falling apart.

'Hi! I see you decided to come home. Does that mean you're feeling better?'

'Yes, thank you.' Her tone was clipped and the churning in his guts intensified.

'Is there something wrong, Rachel?' he demanded, his own voice sounding equally harsh.

'No. I just need some space, time on my own for a change.'

There was no smile to soften the words, nothing but the starkness of the statement, and something warm and tender shrivelled up inside him. Was she tiring of him already, he wondered sickly, wanting to end their relationship so soon? The thought almost brought him to his knees.

'You should have said so this morning if that's how you feel. There was no need to pretend you were ill.'

'As I said, I needed time on my own to think everything through.'

'And now you've had the time you needed, you've come to a decision?'

'Yes. I have.'

'I see.' He shrugged, hoping she couldn't tell how terrified he felt. 'I assume it has something to do with us, so why don't you tell me what you've decided?'

'I think we need to take a break from one another.'

It was what he had feared she'd been going to say and his heart seemed to shrivel up inside him. It was all he could do not to beg her to re-consider but pride dictated that he shouldn't embarrass them both. After all, he had known from the outset that they hadn't promised each other a lifetime of commitment.

'If that's how you feel then there's not a lot I can say, is there?' He shrugged, praying that she couldn't tell how devastated he felt. 'You could be right. Maybe we do need to cool things a bit. It's been very full on recently, hasn't it, Rachel?'

'It has. I…I think we need to take a step back, Matt, don't you?'

There was the tiniest quaver in her voice which gave him some measure of hope that she wasn't convinced about that, but there was nothing to sustain it when he shot a searching look at her face. She looked so distant that it was like looking at a stranger rather than the woman he had grown to love with all his heart.

It seemed too cruel that he had finally admitted how he felt when he was on the point of losing her. Matt knew that he couldn't keep up the pretence any longer and swung round. 'As usual you're spot on in your assessment of the situation, Rachel. I suggest we see how we feel in a couple of weeks' time.'

'I think it would be for the best, too,' she said calmly, and he inwardly cringed as another shaft of pain shot through him. It was hard to believe that she could show so little sign of emotion when he was in such agony.

'I'll take the rest of the day off, if you don't mind,' she continued. 'It will look very odd if I suddenly turn up for work when I'm supposed to be ill.'

'Fine. Do whatever you feel is right.'

Matt went back to his car and got it. Rachel had already closed the door by the time he slipped the key into the ignition and he didn't linger before he drove away. Maybe it was the shock of what had happened but he felt icily cold. He had simply never expected their relationship to end like this. There'd been no tears, no arguments, no recriminations, just a polite indifference that was so much worse. It simply proved how little he had meant to her if Rachel could let him go with so little sign of emotion.

His eyes blurred and he pulled up at the side of the road. Maybe Rachel didn't deem it worth crying about but he did. He had lost the woman he loved for a second time and no matter what happened in the future he would never allow himself to suffer this kind of agony again.

CHAPTER TWELVE

RACHEL sobbed her heart out after Matt had left. It was as though a dam had burst and all the tears she'd been holding back suddenly came gushing out. She felt completely drained afterwards but calmer, better able to think.

She had been right not to tell him just yet that she was pregnant, she realised. The calm and controlled way he had behaved just now had proved that. If he hadn't felt it was worth fighting to keep her then she didn't want him to think that the baby changed anything. She couldn't bear it if Matt felt he had to do the *right* thing. That would be the route to a lifetime of unhappiness for all of them.

The situation was going to be difficult enough as it was. Rachel couldn't imagine how hard it was going to be once the baby was born. Working together each and every day would be a strain for both of them in the circumstances. Although she loved working in Dalverston, it might be better if she found herself a job somewhere else.

The thought of having to start afresh was a daunting one but Rachel knew in her heart it was the right thing to do. What she was going to tell Ross was something she would need to think about, although it could wait for now. Her main concern was to find herself another job as quickly as possible.

She hunted out some back copies of the various medical journals she subscribed to and checked the positions vacant pages. There were a number of possibilities and she marked them all, although her pregnancy could prove a handicap when applying for another post. Most general practices were understaffed and they wouldn't be keen to take on someone who would be able to work for only a few months.

She sighed as she laid the magazines aside. She would deal with that hurdle when she came to it. If nothing else came up, she could always do locum work for a few months to tide her over. She had some savings but they wouldn't last very long if she had to live on them. It could take a while before she sold the cottage and she would have to rent somewhere else in the meantime, so she needed to earn enough to support herself.

Knowing Matt as well as she did, he would probably offer financial support for the baby, although she wasn't sure if she should accept it. The child was her responsibility and she intended to make that clear to him, although she was willing to allow him access if that was what he wanted.

Her heart caught painfully when it struck her that it might be the only time she saw him. The odd couple of hours here and there weren't very much to look forward to after how close they had been, but she knew she had made the right decision. She wouldn't put him under any kind of pressure, wouldn't run the risk of him ending up resenting her. She loved him too much to ruin the rest of his life.

Matt felt as though the rug had been pulled right out from under his feet when Rachel announced that she was looking for another job. In one tiny corner of his mind where hope still resided, he had convinced himself that somehow, some way, they would work through this glitch and come out all the stronger for it on the other side. However, he certainly couldn't see a way out of this. If Rachel left Dalverston that would be the end of them. For good.

'Naturally, I'll work the required period as laid out in my contract. It's two months less any holiday I'm owed.' She consulted her diary. 'That brings it down to six weeks by my reckoning.'

'I'll make a note of that,' he said gruffly, the pain bubbling up inside him so that he had to clamp his teeth together to stop it escaping. He wasn't sure what was worse, the fact that she was planning on leaving or that she could talk about it with so little emotion.

'Don't you want to check that I'm right?' Rachel asked him in surprise, and he shook his head.

'I'm sure you've worked it all out correctly. It's not something you'd make a mistake about, is it?' His tone was brusque but he'd be damned if he would apologise for it. Didn't she know how hard this was for him, didn't she even care?

'No, it isn't.'

There was the tiniest hint of a plea in her voice but he wasn't going to make the mistake of thinking she was asking for his understanding. She had made up her mind what she intended to do and she didn't give a damn about the effect it would have on him.

He stood up abruptly. 'I take it that you'll be applying for another post?'

'Yes. I've already seen a couple of jobs that look suitable,' she agreed, digging in the knife that bit further. She certainly wasn't wasting any time, he thought savagely. Obviously, she was keen to put some distance between them as soon as she possibly could!

'I see,' he said, clamping down on the emotions that were churning around inside him. He would be damned if he'd let her know how angry and hurt he felt, especially when she didn't care. He shrugged, feigning an indifference he wished he felt. 'It goes without saying that I'll be happy to provide you with a reference. You've done an excellent job while you've been here, Rachel. Any practice will be lucky to have you as part of their team.'

'Thank you.'

Her voice caught on the words but Matt didn't wait to see what had caused it. His control was held by a thread and he was desperate not to embarrass himself in front of her. He went to the door, pausing briefly to glance back, but she wasn't looking at him. She was staring down at her diary, probably counting the days until she could shake off the dust of her old life in Dalverston and set off on a new adventure somewhere else.

Had it been their ill-fated affair that had pushed her into making the move? he wondered bitterly, then hurriedly blanked out the answer. He didn't want to know if *he* was responsible for driving her away.

* * *

'*Leaving?*'

'Yes.' Rachel summoned a smile but it wasn't easy when she felt so devastated inside. 'I know it's probably come as a shock to you, darling…'

'Too damned right it has!' Ross slumped down onto a chair and stared at her in bewilderment. 'Why on earth do you want to leave? I thought you loved it here in Dalverston.'

'I do…I mean, I did, but recently I've had the feeling that I'm stuck in a bit of a rut.' She perched on the edge of the sofa, willing her son to accept her explanation without probing too deeply. The last thing she wanted was Ross discovering the truth at this stage, although he would have to know at some point.

'This hasn't anything to do with Matt, has it? You two haven't…well, fallen out?'

'What do you mean?' she asked in surprise, flushing when Ross gave her a speaking look.

'There's no point denying it, Mum. It was

obvious that you two were an item at Christmas.'

'I…um…was it?'

'Yes, and before you ask, I was delighted for you both.' He leant forward. 'It's about time the pair of you thought about yourselves for a change. I really like Matt and to my mind you two are ideally suited. If something has happened, are you sure you can't work it out between you?'

'I'm afraid not. That's one of the reasons why I've decided I need to make some changes to my life, although it's not the only reason.' For a moment she was tempted to tell him about the baby but it would be wrong to tell Ross before she told Matt and then expect him to keep her secret. She hurried on, trying to put a positive spin on her plans.

'I'm not getting any younger, Ross, and if I don't make the move now then I'll never do it. I don't want to end up regretting it in a few years' time.'

'Is that the truth?' Ross demanded.

Rachel felt herself colour when she heard the scepticism in his voice even though it was true in a way. If she stayed in Dalverston she could cause untold problems for Matt and that was something she would regret bitterly for the rest of her life. 'Yes. Of course it's true!' she exclaimed with, hopefully, a convincing amount of indignation. 'Do you really think I would lie to you?'

'Sorry, of course you wouldn't.' Ross sighed. 'It's just that I can't bear to think that you're leaving because of some sort of silly misunderstanding that could very well be cleared up.'

'I'm not. I've thought long and hard about this decision and I know it's the right thing to do.' She quickly changed the subject, afraid that she would let something slip if Ross kept pushing her. 'Anyway, enough about me. How are you and Gemma getting on?'

'Great! I never thought I'd feel like this about anyone. I'm head over heels in love with her.'

'I'm so happy for you, Ross,' Rachel said sincerely.

'Are you? I was afraid you'd think it was too soon after what happened with Heather…' He stopped abruptly, looking deeply concerned. 'I hope it wasn't that which caused you and Matt to split up? I've no idea how he feels about me and Gemma seeing each other because he's never said anything to me. But it can't be easy for him to accept that I've met someone else so soon. I do hope I haven't caused a rift between you two.'

'You haven't,' she said firmly. 'I can say with my hand on my heart that me breaking up with Matt had nothing whatsoever to do with you, darling.'

'Thanks heavens for that!' Ross laughed

ruefully. 'I'd hate to think that I had caused you a whole load of grief at my age.'

'You have never caused me any problems at any age,' she told him truthfully. 'Having you was the best thing that ever happened to me, darling. Believe me, it's true.'

'And you are the best mother in the world.'

Ross stood up and hugged her. He seemed a lot happier after that, eager to hear about the plans she had made. Rachel told him what she could, carefully avoiding any outright lies. She would tell him about the baby once all the tests had been done and everything was clear. How he would take the news was open to question but she would deal with that when it arose.

Ross left a short time later, promising to do all he could to help make the move as stress-free as possible for her. Rachel locked up and went upstairs to bed, wishing with all her heart it was as simple as that. Leaving her home and her job would have been stressful enough but factor in all the rest—Matt and the baby—and the stress factor achieved whole new levels. However, she would cope because she had to. She would cope because it was the right thing to do. She wouldn't trap Matt into a situation he wouldn't welcome, although she couldn't help thinking wistfully how different things might have been if they had been truly committed to one another when she had found out she was pregnant. They could have had something to celebrate then.

Matt felt as though he was caught up in some terrible nightmare. Every day that passed brought the day when Rachel might leave ever closer and he had no idea how he was going to cope when it happened. What made it worse was that she was so distant with him, confining any contact they had to strictly work-related matters. After their recent closeness, he felt her withdrawal all the more keenly and couldn't understand it.

Why had she changed her mind about him so suddenly? One minute she had seemed as blissfully happy as he had been and the next she hadn't wanted anything to do with him. The more he thought about it the stranger it appeared and he knew that he wouldn't rest until he found out what had gone wrong. It was having the opportunity to ask her that was the problem. There was no time to discuss it at work—she made sure they were never together long enough to give him the opportunity. As for going to see her after work, he knew it would be a waste of time— she would probably refuse to speak to him. No, he needed to find a time and a place when she couldn't avoid him.

He finally got his chance one evening. Carol had organised a fortieth birthday 'do' after work—dinner and drinks at a local pub—for Dianne, the newest member of their reception team. Matt had no intention of going when it was first mentioned to him. Quite frankly, the last thing he felt like doing was celebrating, so he made an excuse. However, when he discovered on the day that Rachel was going, he changed his mind. It could be his one and only chance to talk to her. After all, she could hardly ignore him with everyone there watching them.

Carol was standing at the bar when he arrived that night. She smiled in delight when she saw him coming in. 'Oh, wonderful, you've decided to come after all.' She pointed towards the far side of the room. 'We've managed to grab ourselves a table over there. What do you want to drink? I'm just about to order.'

'Oh, just a bottle of beer for me, please.' He took out his wallet and handed her several twenty-pound notes. 'Here, use this.'

Carol whistled. 'That's very generous of

you, Matt. I'm doubly glad you managed to get here now!'

Matt laughed dutifully then made his way across the room, replying automatically to the friendly greetings that met him. Rachel was sitting in the corner and he frowned when he saw how pale and drawn she looked. She smiled politely as he pulled out a chair, but he could see the alarm in her eyes and knew that he was the last person she'd expected to see. 'Hello, Matt. I didn't know you were coming.'

'I wasn't planning to, but I changed my mind at the last minute.' He leant forward, subjecting her to a searching look. 'Are you sure you should be here, though? You look worn out.'

His eyes held hers fast although he had no idea what she could see on his face at that moment. All of a sudden he didn't give a damn either. This might be his only chance to sort out this mess and he refused to waste it by pretending he didn't care.

He did care, he cared a lot, loved her too, and only wished he could tell her that. The fact that she was unlikely to welcome such an admission was incidental. It didn't stop him feeling how he did. He loved her more than life itself and if there was any way to make her understand that she was wrong to leave him then, by heaven, he'd find it.

'It…it's been rather hectic in work lately, hasn't it? I expect that's why I'm looking so tired.'

Rachel could feel her heart pounding as she looked away from Matt's probing gaze. She had only agreed to come because Carol had told her that Matt wouldn't be there, so it had been a shock to see him coming into the pub. She cast him a wary look from under her eyelashes and felt her breath catch when she discovered that he was still watching her. She had no idea what was going on but the expression on his face stunned her. Why was he looking at her as though he genuinely cared?

'Okey-dokey, folks, it's drinkie time! Here you go, Rachel. A nice big G&T to perk you up and put some colour in your cheeks.'

Carol came back with a loaded tray and plonked a glass down in front of her. She held up her hand when Rachel opened her mouth to protest it wasn't what she had ordered. 'Forget it. There is no way that you're having orange juice tonight. We're here to celebrate Dianne's birthday and you need a proper drink to do that!'

Rachel summoned a smile when everyone cheered, but she could have done without this. She couldn't drink alcohol in her condition, although how she could avoid it without causing a fuss was another matter. Picking up the glass, she pretended to take a sip. 'Mmm, that's delicious.'

'Good. Get it down you, then. There's plenty more where that came from, courtesy of our beloved leader.'

Carol looked pointedly at Matt and Rachel realised that with typical generosity he must have paid for their drinks. Once everyone had a glass in front of them, Fraser stood up and proposed a toast.

'To Dianne and the next forty years. May they be filled with health, wealth and happiness.'

Everyone raised their glasses aloft. Rachel went to pick up her drink and gasped when the glass suddenly flew across the table. Gin and tonic went everywhere, causing pandemonium as they all leapt out of the way.

'Sorry, sorry! My fault,' Matt apologised, grabbing a handful of paper napkins and hurriedly mopping up the mess. 'I must have knocked the glass over when I went to pick up my bottle of beer.' He glanced at Rachel. 'I'll get you another one.'

He got up and went to the bar, returning a few minutes later with a fresh glass. Placing it carefully on a coaster, he smiled at her. 'Try that. It should be just right for you.'

Rachel cautiously raised the glass to her lips, feeling shock run through her when she tasted the sharp, undiluted bitterness of pure tonic water. How had he guessed that she didn't want to drink any alcohol? she wondered giddily. Surely he didn't suspect that she was pregnant?

The thought made her insides churn with apprehension and she hastily excused herself as she headed to the ladies' lavatories. Although the bouts of morning sickness had tailed off, there were times throughout the day when she felt nauseous and this was one of them. She sluiced her face with cold water then sat on the little stool in front of the vanity bench and took several deep breaths, feeling better as her panic started to subside. There was nothing the least significant about Matt buying her that drink. He had simply heard Carol's comment about her asking for a non-alcoholic drink and with typical thoughtfulness he had taken account of that. There was certainly no reason to believe that he had guessed she was pregnant.

Rachel stood up, feeling calmer now that she had reasoned everything out. She opened the door to go back and join the others, and came to an abrupt halt when she saw Matt leaning against the wall. It was obvious that he was waiting for her and her stomach lurched once again as she found herself wondering what he wanted.

All of a sudden it was just too much for her to deal with. With a tiny moan, she fled back into the toilets and was violently sick. Crouching down on the floor of the stall, she closed her eyes in despair. Even if Matt hadn't worked out already that she was pregnant, it wouldn't take him long to do so!

CHAPTER THIRTEEN

MATT could feel the shock wave spreading up from his toes. It reached his knees, moved up to his hips, his chest and finally arrived at his brain. He closed his eyes, desperately trying to find another explanation for what had happened that night but he really couldn't think of one. Was it possible that Rachel was pregnant?

His eyes flew open again because he just knew it was true. It explained so much that had made no sense before. Rachel was expecting a baby, his baby, and that was why she had decided to leave Dalverston. It hadn't anything to do with her lack of feelings for him—well, hopefully, not—she had just got it into her head that it was the right thing to do. He could actually understand her reasoning now that he thought about it: they hadn't made a commitment; she had no idea how he really felt about her; she was far too proud to make it appear as though she was using the baby to *force* him into staying with her—as if that would have been necessary!

Matt pushed open the restroom door, his heart aching when he saw her crouched on the floor of the nearest stall. He knelt down beside her and drew her into his arms, knowing that he would never forgive himself for putting her through this ordeal. 'It's all right, sweetheart. Everything is going to be fine, I promise you that.'

'How can it be?' she whispered, raising tear-drenched eyes to his.

'Because there's no problem in the world that we can't solve so long as we do it together.' He brushed the damp curls off her forehead. 'You, me and our baby.'

Her eyes widened in shock. 'How did you guess?'

'It wasn't that difficult.' He kissed her gently on the cheek. 'I am a doctor, don't forget— I've been trained to recognise the signs.'

'I'm so sorry, Matt. I never meant it to happen. I just didn't think that it would when we were always so careful.'

Her voice rose on a wail and he pulled her closer, rocking her to and fro while she sobbed out all the fear and heartache of the last few weeks. Matt couldn't bear to imagine what she must have been through and blamed himself for it too. If only he'd told her how much he loved her then none of this would have happened.

He waited until she was a little calmer then urged her to her feet. 'Let's get out of here. We need to talk, Rachel, and we can't do it in here, can we?'

'But what about the others?' she protested as he steered her along the passageway that led out to the car park. 'They'll think it's very odd if we just up and leave without saying anything.'

'What people think is the least of my worries,' he said firmly, unlocking the car and helping her inside. He dropped a kiss on her forehead then fastened her seat belt for her. 'Anyway, I doubt we'll be missed for very long. They'll be too busy celebrating.'

'Well, if you're sure it's all right…'

'It will be fine. Don't worry.' He tilted her face up to his and kissed her lips. 'We have more important things to think about.'

'I don't want you to feel that you have to do anything you don't want to do,' she began, and he sighed softly as he placed a gentle finger against her lips.

'I don't, so you can get that idea right out of your head.' He looked deep into her eyes. 'I love you, Rachel. I only wish I'd told you that sooner but I was too afraid to admit how I felt to myself or to you.'

'You love me?' she whispered, her eyes enormous as she stared back at him.

'Yes. Now, let's go home and see if we can sort this all out.'

Rachel nodded mutely. She appeared too stunned to say anything. Matt got into the car and drove them back to his house, hoping that he had managed to convince her he was telling the truth. He couldn't bear it if she thought he had only said he loved her because of the baby, when it wasn't true.

The thought nagged away at him as he ushered her into the sitting room. The fire had died down so he added a fresh log and soon had it blazing away. His breath caught as he turned and saw how beautiful Rachel looked with the firelight bringing out the chestnut glints in her hair. He loved her more than life itself and there was no way that he was prepared to lose her.

'Would you like something to drink?' he asked as his resolve hardened.

'A cup of tea would be nice,' she said quietly, not quite meeting his eyes. 'Although I'd like to brush my teeth first, if you don't mind.'

'Of course I don't mind. You know where everything is, so help yourself.'

'Thank you.' She started towards the door, stopped and turned back. 'About the baby, Matt—'

'Later. We'll talk about everything once you've tidied yourself up.' He closed the gap between them and dropped a gentle kiss on her cheek. 'Just remember that I love you, Rachel, and that nothing will ever change that.'

'I had no idea,' she whispered.

'How could you have known when I made such a good job of hiding my feelings?' He rubbed the pad of his thumb along her jaw and felt her tremble. His confidence soared because it proved she wasn't indifferent to him.

'I only wish I'd told you the truth before now, then we could have avoided all this upset.'

'I never gave you the chance to say how you felt about anything,' she said, her voice catching. 'It's not your fault, Matt, it's mine. All of it.'

'It's nobody's fault,' he said firmly. He kissed her again then headed to the kitchen and set about making the tea. Rachel hadn't said how she felt about him yet, but he refused to believe that she didn't care about him. The fact that she intended to have his baby proved that she did.

He smiled as he dropped tea bags into the pot. From now on life was going to be very different. There would be no more holding back, no more guilt, definitely no regrets. He would embrace the future and what lay in store for them all—him, Rachel and their son or daughter.

* * *

Rachel sighed she made her way back down the stairs a short time later. Matt's reaction to the news that she was pregnant had stunned her. She was very much aware that she had done him a grave injustice. She had simply assumed that he would be upset about the baby instead of letting him tell her how he felt himself. It just seemed to confirm how little she really knew about relationships.

It was an unsettling thought and it was hard to shrug it off as she went into the sitting room. Matt had poured their tea and placed the cups on the table in front of the fire. Rachel sat down on the sofa, feeling incredibly nervous as she picked up her cup and saucer. It wasn't just Matt's reaction to her being pregnant that had shocked her, of course. She'd been stunned when he had told her that he loved her. Although she desperately wanted to believe him, she couldn't help having doubts. What if he had only told her that because he'd felt it was the right thing to do in the circumstances?

The cup clattered back onto its saucer and she saw Matt look at her. Even though it was tempting just to accept what he said, she knew in her heart that she needed to be absolutely sure about his feelings for her. 'I don't want you to feel that you have to… well, pretend, Matt.'

'What do you mean?'

'You said that you loved me but are you sure that it's true? You're not just saying that because of the baby?'

'No, I'm not!' he exclaimed forcefully. 'I know it's taken me a long time to admit it but I love you, and it has nothing to do with the fact that you're having my baby.'

Rachel's heart overflowed with happiness when she heard the conviction in his voice. 'You can't imagine how wonderful it feels to hear you say that and know that you mean it.'

'Oh, I think I can.' He smiled at her with a wealth of tenderness in his eyes. 'I can imagine only too well how marvellous it must feel to know that you're loved.'

Rachel knew what he was asking her and all of a sudden it was the simplest thing in the world to give him the answer he wanted. 'You don't need to imagine it any longer because it's true. I love you, Matt. So very, very much.'

'Wow!' He laughed deeply. 'It feels even better than I thought it would, especially as I'd convinced myself that you didn't care a fig about me after you announced that you were leaving Dalverston.'

'I never wanted to leave,' she admitted. 'I just thought it was the right thing to do.'

'Because you didn't know how I'd feel about becoming a father again?'

'Yes. I…I thought you'd be horrified and I was afraid that you would end up hating me.'

'I could never hate you,' he said so sincerely that it brought tears to her eyes. He leant forward and she saw fleeting sadness cross his face. 'If I hadn't found out tonight by accident, would you have left without saying anything?'

'No! I always intended to tell you about the baby, Matt. I just decided that it would be better if we weren't together at the time. That way you wouldn't feel as though you had to stay with me for the sake of our child. I didn't want you to feel trapped.'

He shook his head. 'I would never have felt like that, Rachel. I'm thrilled to bits that I'm going to be a dad again.'

'You really mean that, don't you?' She smiled at him, uncaring that tears were streaming down her cheeks.

'Of course I do.' He came and knelt in front of her, his face filled with wonderment as he placed his hand ever so gently on her stomach. 'The thought that there is a new life growing in there all because of our love for each other is just so wonderful. Thank you, Rachel. Thank you so much for giving me such a marvellous gift.'

'There's no guarantee the pregnancy will go to term,' she said quickly. Even though she didn't want anything to spoil this moment for them, she had to be honest about the risks involved. 'I'll need to have all kinds of tests done because of my age…'

'I realise that. But no matter what happens, darling, it won't change how I feel. It couldn't do. I love you and I want to be with you for ever. This baby is just a wonderful bonus.'

He kissed her softly on the lips, a kiss of great tenderness that quickly turned to one of passion. Rachel kissed him back, wanting him to know how much she loved him. They made love right there on the rug in front of the fire, their bodies warmed by the blaze as well as the heat of their desire. Rachel's heart overflowed with happiness as she gave herself up to Matt's tender ministrations and allowed all the misery of the past few weeks to melt away. She would never ever doubt him again. She knew now in her heart that he would always be true to her, that he loved her and wanted her for evermore. Maybe that was the key to a lasting relationship, she thought in surprise: trust. She had never trusted anyone before but she trusted Matt and nothing that happened from this moment on would destroy that trust.

It was a moment of revelation she would remember for the rest of her life, a life she would share with Matt and their child, hopefully. When they finally drew apart she told him that and saw the tears that shimmered in his eyes as he realised she was giving him another precious gift. He kissed her hungrily then drew her close, pulling a throw off the sofa and covering them with it so that they were cocooned in their happiness and she couldn't begin to explain how it made her feel, safe, secure, loved. She had the whole world right here, she thought dreamily, everything she wanted and needed. How lucky she was.

Matt felt a wave of relief wash away the nightmare that he had lived with for weeks. There wasn't a doubt in his mind that Rachel had meant it when she had said that she loved him and he couldn't describe how it made him feel. To know that this beautiful, caring woman wanted him for ever and ever was too much to take in. He kissed her hair, feeling the silky waves clinging to his lips. He had been given the rarest, most precious gift of all: he was loved.

'What are you thinking?'

He tipped his head to the side and smiled at

her. 'That I'm the luckiest man alive to be loved by you.'

'And I'm the luckiest woman alive to be loved by *you*,' she replied softly, kissing the side of his jaw.

'Hmm, that feels so good,' he murmured, drawing her closer so that she could feel exactly how good it had been, and she giggled, a girlish, happy sound that filled him with delight.

'You are insatiable, Matthew Thompson!'

'Guilty as charged,' he replied, nibbling her bare shoulder. 'I'm not going to argue with you, so does that win me any extra brownie points?'

'No, it doesn't…well, maybe a few,' she relented as he drew her even closer. 'However, I think we need to finish our talk before we tot up how many points you've scored.'

'About us and the baby, you mean?' He lay back on the rug, drawing her into his arms so that her head was cushioned on his bare chest. 'That's easy. Obviously, we're going to get married and live happily ever after…'

'Whoa! Hang on a second.' She sat up and stared at him. 'Did you say married?'

'Of course.' He ran a finger down her cheek, let it flow on towards her collar bone, his intentions clear until she grabbed hold of his hand.

'There is no "of course" about it! Marriage is a huge commitment.'

'So is having a baby and we're doing that, aren't we?' He smiled up at her. 'Call me old-fashioned, Rachel, but I believe in marriage. I think it's the best basis for two people who want to build a life together. It also offers stability when there are children involved.'

'Hmph! You make it sound very romantic. What happened to love and lust, etcetera?'

'Oh, there will be lots of that!' He pulled her down beside him and gently rolled her onto her back then kissed her lips. 'I want to marry you because I love you, because I want to spend the rest of my life with you. I want to know that you're mine and that no matter what happens we'll always be together.'

He kissed her lingeringly, savouring the sweetness of her mouth. It was an effort to continue when he finally drew back. 'I also swear on my honour that once we are married I shall see it as my duty to keep lust alive and fully functioning. I definitely don't intend to take you for granted if that's what you're worried about.'

'It did cross my mind,' she said, grinning shamelessly up at him.

'Then don't let it cross it again.' He rose to his knees and took hold of her hand. 'So will you marry me, Rachel Mackenzie, and make me the happiest as well as the luckiest man in the world?'

'I'll need to think about it,' she replied, pretending to give the idea due thought. She squealed when he pulled her into his arms and kissed her soundly. 'All right, then, yes! Yes, I'll marry you, Matt, although what Heather and Ross are going to think about us getting married is anyone's guess.'

'They'll be thrilled to bits, especially when they find out about the baby,' he assured her with a confidence that stemmed from pure joy. Nothing would spoil their happiness. He wouldn't let it!

'Let's hope they are both up for a spot of babysitting,' Rachel murmured, pulling him towards her.

That marked the end of the conversation, not that Matt was sorry. They had far better things to do and they did them too. As they lay together in his bed later that night, he felt as though he was floating on air. He had found the woman who was going to make his world complete again and they were having a child. Life couldn't get any better than this!

Two years later....

A soft breeze blew in off the ocean, cooling the heat of the day to a bearable level. Matt stood beside the platform that had been built above the shore and watched the waves lapping at the glistening white sand. It was his wedding day and he knew that it was going to be a very special occasion, one he and Rachel would remember for the rest of their lives with pleasure.

They had flown to Thailand at the beginning of the week and spent several days in Bangkok completing the formalities. Once that was done they and their guests had been driven to Hua Hin on the coast. Rachel had confessed that it had always been her dream to be married by the ocean and he had pulled out all the stops to make sure that she had the wedding she wanted. It was winter back home in England but here in this tropical paradise the sun shone each and every day. Another wonderful omen for their life together.

The music suddenly changed, the triumphant strains of the Wedding March heralding his bride's arrival. Matt turned to face her, feeling his heart overflow with love. She had been very secretive about her dress and had forbidden him to take even the tiniest peek at it, but it had been worth the wait. Rachel looked a vision in the simple silk gown she had chosen for the occasion with tiny, star-like white flowers in her hair.

His smiled at her then let his gaze move on to the people who had travelled all that way to celebrate them getting married. Heather was here with her husband, Archie, both of them looking so gloriously happy that Matt's own pleasure intensified. Ross was also here with Gemma at his side and it was obvious that they were very much in love too. Ben and Zoe were laughing as they held hands with their daughter, who was skipping along beside them. They too had the look that all couples in love shared, one of happiness and pride. How odd that a cancelled wedding had led to so many people finding true love.

'Dada!'

Matt's smiled widened when he recognised a familiar little voice. He stepped forward and lifted the little girl out of her mother's arms. Sophie Jane Thompson was the image of her mother from her shiny chestnut curls to her huge brown eyes and he adored her.

'Hello, princess. Have you been a good girl for Mummy?'

Sophie nodded her head, setting the tiny flowers that had been woven through her hair bobbing. She was wearing a white dress too, with frilly white socks and white satin shoes. Matt put her down on the ground and took a firm hold of her hand as he smiled at Rachel.

'You look beautiful,' he said softly, loving her with his eyes.

'Thank you,' she replied, smiling up at him as she slipped her hand into his. 'Not changed your mind, have you? You still want to go ahead with this?'

'Oh, most definitely.'

He dropped a kiss on her lips then led her towards the arch of flowers that marked the entrance to the podium that had been erected for the ceremony. There was a muslin canopy overhead to shade them from the sun and more flowers arranged in huge vividly coloured displays, but Matt was barely aware of his surroundings as he made his vows to love and cherish Rachel until the day he died.

This was what mattered most, he thought. These promises they made. He meant every word and knew that Rachel meant them too, and happiness filled him to the brim. They were going to have the most wonderful life together.

MEDICAL™

Large Print

Titles for the next six months…

August

EMERGENCY: PARENTS NEEDED	Jessica Matthews
A BABY TO CARE FOR	Lucy Clark
PLAYBOY SURGEON, TOP-NOTCH DAD	Janice Lynn
ONE SUMMER IN SANTA FE	Molly Evans
ONE TINY MIRACLE…	Carol Marinelli
MIDWIFE IN A MILLION	Fiona McArthur

September

THE DOCTOR'S LOST-AND-FOUND BRIDE	Kate Hardy
MIRACLE: MARRIAGE REUNITED	Anne Fraser
A MOTHER FOR MATILDA	Amy Andrews
THE BOSS AND NURSE ALBRIGHT	Lynne Marshall
NEW SURGEON AT ASHVALE A&E	Joanna Neil
DESERT KING, DOCTOR DADDY	Meredith Webber

October

THE NURSE'S BROODING BOSS	Laura Iding
EMERGENCY DOCTOR AND CINDERELLA	Melanie Milburne
CITY SURGEON, SMALL TOWN MIRACLE	Marion Lennox
BACHELOR DAD, GIRL NEXT DOOR	Sharon Archer
A BABY FOR THE FLYING DOCTOR	Lucy Clark
NURSE, NANNY…BRIDE!	Alison Roberts

MILLS & BOON®

MEDICAL™

Large Print

November

THE SURGEON'S MIRACLE	Caroline Anderson
DR DI ANGELO'S BABY BOMBSHELL	Janice Lynn
NEWBORN NEEDS A DAD	Dianne Drake
HIS MOTHERLESS LITTLE TWINS	Dianne Drake
WEDDING BELLS FOR THE VILLAGE NURSE	Abigail Gordon
HER LONG-LOST HUSBAND	Josie Metcalfe

December

THE MIDWIFE AND THE MILLIONAIRE	Fiona McArthur
FROM SINGLE MUM TO LADY	Judy Campbell
KNIGHT ON THE CHILDREN'S WARD	Carol Marinelli
CHILDREN'S DOCTOR, SHY NURSE	Molly Evans
HAWAIIAN SUNSET, DREAM PROPOSAL	Joanna Neil
RESCUED: MOTHER AND BABY	Anne Fraser

January

DARE SHE DATE THE DREAMY DOC?	Sarah Morgan
DR DROP-DEAD GORGEOUS	Emily Forbes
HER BROODING ITALIAN SURGEON	Fiona Lowe
A FATHER FOR BABY ROSE	Margaret Barker
NEUROSURGEON…AND MUM!	Kate Hardy
WEDDING IN DARLING DOWNS	Leah Martyn